Twin Mi-Chi

Part - 1

Manav Jain

Invincible Publishers

Published by

Invincible Publishers

201A, SAS Tower, Sector 38,

Gurugram – 122003

Phone: 01244034247, +91-9599667779

Web: www.invinciblepublishers.com

First Published in 2020

ISBN: 978-81-945481-8-8

Printed at: Thomson Press India

Acknowledgement

In my past, writing was not my zone, but today, I managed to pen down an entire novel. And the very fact of me writing a book is still unbelievable. First, a big bow to my Grandfather Mr. Nainmalji Heerachandji because of whom I have reached to this level. Second, my loving Mom Mrs. Anita Kumari and caring Dad Mr. Lalit Kumar. Their support and love have raised me to a position they are proud of. I am immensely grateful to my Brothers; Mr. Gagan Jain and his spouse Mrs. Pooja and Mr.Vivek Jain his spouse Mrs. Ashika for their constant support.

I owe gratitude to my beloved wife Meghana, my Daughter Sayana and my in-laws for always being around and motivating me to pen down this book. A special thanks to my sister Vaishali for being the first reader and for her appraisal of the book. I am thankful to the team of Invincible Publishers for their intense efforts and making my manuscript turn into a beautiful paperback.

Contents

Part – I

Part – II

Chapter 1
The Faceoff

Dark clouds were wandering in the sky with a lot of thundering. Alien (Zexox) stood on the spacecraft and was waiting for Krum to kill Shankar and then attack planet earth; it was a faceoff between Shankar and Krum. Shankar was trying to kill Krum because he had already destroyed many places with the help of Zexox and was unstoppable. On the other hand, Shankar stood with intense looks. He created a gadget in a lab that could re-size any non-living object and pull any small object and resize it. He was also a very good martial artist, learned by his master Vu. Zexox had a deal with Krum that if Krum killed Shankar and handed over the device to him, then he would be his partner in ruling the earth together. If lost, he would have to go back to his place. Shankar had a device by which he would have destroyed Zexox. However, it was only possible for him to destroy Zexox if he was near Zexox's main chamber, where the remote would be activated with the switch. The Switch had an image in it which had to be matched and then pressed. Switch image Shown below.

The fight began and Shankar ran towards Krum. He then took a needle from the gadget and threw it in front of Krum and made the needle turn huge. Krum saw the needle turning huge and thus jumped and used his weapon to hit the object towards the ground. Be that as it may, Shankar reached Krum and hit him hard on the face. Shankar was very strong on Krum and was not letting him overcome, but at the moment, Zexox threw a small marble ball towards Krum and then Krum rolled it in front of Shankar who was looking in the other direction, saving a small girl who unknowingly came in between. When Shankar turned around, he saw a big metal ball with spikes coming in his way. The ball was huge enough to crush any object. Shankar anyhow dogged the ball and got a scratch on his right shoulder. He covered his wound with his left hand and stood contemplating whether he should go ahead to save the people by stopping the ball or to kill Krum. He decided to save the people and thus ran towards the ball shouting; "move aside, the ball is unstoppable." Shankar reached a limit near the ball where his gadget could work and make the ball turn small. With the help of his gadget, the ball became small and he then pulled it towards him, turned around and threw the ball towards Zexox and resized it. The ball moving towards Zexox passed through Krum and finally reached Zexox. Zexox was so powerful that he used his ring's power and turned the direction of the ball which then flew above him and hit another spacecraft and was destroyed. Suddenly, Krum used his speed run power (a ring's power by which he could run fast), ran swiftly and came near Shankar. He took the benefit of diversion, caught Shankar's neck and stared sharply in his eyes, stating, "now, what are you going to do?" Shankar, in pain tried to punch Krum, but Krum caught Shankar's hand and broke the Gadget by crushing his hand. Shankar screamed in pain. Krum then used another ring's power to pull his weapon (a weapon which was interlinked with the ring) towards him and laughed, Ha ha ha ha. He said, "Now, how are you going to save the Earth? Don't worry, I am not going to kill you. We will keep you alive and hurt you daily by killing your people in front of your eyes."

Shankar, with no fear in his eyes, looked at Krum and replied, "Kill me now or you will regret later."

Zexox said, "What are you doing? Finish this ant and bring the device to me." Krum looked at Zexox, and in the meantime Shankar kicked Krum in the stomach. Krum screamed in pain, still holding Shankar and saw him angrily. He stabbed Shankar's stomach in sheer anger with his weapon. Shankar screamed, "aaahhhh..." Krum threw Shankar and walked away.

Shankar rolled on the ground facing the sky with a lot of blood flowing from his stomach. Seeing him in such intense pain, Raman could not stop himself and came running towards Shankar. Raman then sat down, lifted Shankar and made him lay on his lap. He then tore Shankar's shirt and covered the wound with the cloth and said, "Do not close your eyes, we will heal you." Shankar's eyes were filled with tears. Raman brought his hand under Shankar's face, not letting the tears fall on ground and then said, "These tears are not supposed to fall on the ground," and gave him strength. While Krum and Zexox were celebrating Shankar's defeat, Shankar took the opportunity and got up slowly to reach Raman's ear and said, "send a message to the Aries king JOI to attack Zexox's planet." He also handed him a remote switch, asking to split the switch into two so that Zexox could not find it. Raman called a few known members from the crowd and asked them to hide Shankar and to replace the remote by a duplicate one and carry the original remote with Shankar. He left the duplicate remote on the ground so that the enemies would get distracted. Raman got up and ran towards his vehicle, carrying the original switch to Shankar's wife.

Raman reached Shankar's home and started banging the door. He shouted, "Swati, are you home? Please open the door." Swati came quickly and opened the door. Seeing Raman's hands soaked in blood, she asked him, "where is Shankar and what happened?" Raman, with tears in his eyes informed her about the situation and said, "Don't worry,

Shankar is safe. He is with our people. They hid Shankar in a place where the enemies could not find him."

Zexox and Krum thought that Shankar would never get up. However, to their great surprise, when they looked for him, he was missing and the other people were also missing. They searched in all places but couldn't find them. While searching, they found the remote on the ground. Krum ordered his servant, "bring the remote to me."

Krum took the remote to Zexox and then both started celebrating their victory, without knowing that the remote was duplicate and the switch was missing. He gave the remote to his chief and said, "safeguard it."

Zexox then ordered the chief to attack the planet. The chief went inside the chamber and was about to attack the planet, but he suddenly screamed and came running towards Zexox. Gasping for breath, he uttered, "Sir, I cannot find the switch, the remote is a duplicate."

Zexox replied, "What?"

Zexox became angry because the switch was missing from the remote and on the other hand, he received a message from the chief of the planet saying, "Sir, our planet is under Attack by Aries king JOI." Hearing that, he left by saying, "I will come back and destroy the planet." He then commanded Krum, "Find the switch and Shankar as soon as possible." He then flew to safeguard his planet.Krum's men, who followed Raman silently, called Krum and informed, "The switch was taken to Swati." Krum then went in search of her.

In the meantime, at Shankar's house, Swati was screaming in pain, "My water bag is broken." As she was pregnant, Raman called his doctor friend and informed about the situation. They both then made a full proof plan to exchange Swati with another lady and take her to his private lab. Raman then interchanged Swati with another lady acting as Swati in the ambulance and also kept a note for Shankar. He shifted Swati from the ambulance to a van.

Shankar was safe with the people trying to heal him as quickly as possible so that he could go to Swati and take the switch. Swati was not taken to the hospital as Krum was searching for her. She was taken to another place where the delivery could take place. Krum went to Shankar's house and started searching for Swati. He broke all the furniture and messed up the house. While searching, he got a note which was written for Shankar, "Sorry, Shankar. Swati was not able to wait for you to come, so I am taking her to Apex hospital for delivery. Meet me there." Krum and his men took their vehicle to find the ambulance. It was raining heavily and therefore the ambulance was stuck in the middle of the road. Krum found the ambulance, broke the door and found Swati (Exchanged lady). He gave her an angry look and said, "nor you or your upcoming child will see tomorrow's sunlight." Krum took the lady along with him to a safe house, tortured her asking about the switch and Shankar. Krum, in full anger walked towards her and slapped her. He then pulled her hair and asked, "where is the switch?" The lady replied, "you better kill me. I am not going to say anything about it." Krum, in frustration turned back and started walking towards the exit. His eyes went down and he saw a locket laying on the ground. When he picked it up, he got to know that the lady was a hoax. Krum became angrier and stabbed the lady, but it was pillow and he then threw the lady by holding her hair. The lady then got up and said, "An Evil like you will never get what you need. Shankar will end your life and you will not be able even to touch him."

She bit Krum and tried to escape, but Krum's men caught her and said, "now, we will keep you alive and you will have to see the hell on earth." She was then handed over to aliens and they kept her as their slave by torturing her. Krum's man, who was following Raman, called Krum through a P.C.O and asked, "Sir, where are you?" Before he could ask another question, Krum shouted at him and said, "You fool, where did you go when I reached Shankar's home and why are you not picking up the call?"

The man replied, "Sorry, sir. My phone fell on the road while following Raman, so I was not able to contact you."

Then he gave Krum the information about the place and also said, "Sir, Swati has delivered twin babies; the boy is named Chirag (he had fire in his eyes) and the girl is named Chiara (she had blossom eyes which could make anyone fall in love with her)." *Only the names were stated, not the powers gifted.

Krum went along with his men to get the switch. He reached the spot and entered the doctor's lab. Krum's men caught everyone present there by pointing a gun on them. Krum walked towards Swati and said, "Well, well, well, finally, all the hide and seek is over and I caught you. I won."

Krum held the face of Swati. Raman shouted, "Don't you dare touch her."

Krum – "Shut up, you swine. I will come to you also, don't worry." Krum then saw that Swati was unconscious.

Krum to his men – "Gather all the people at one place and hit them till I say no."

After a few minutes, Krum said to his men, "Ok, ok, now stop. Come to me, let me show you people something." Krum walked in style towards the babies. He saw two cute twins and laughed at them, saying, "What time you have come in this world and now you will be going back soon." The moment he came closer to the girl child, he picked her up and saw in her eyes. Krum was blossomed and fell in love with her. She had the power to make anyone fall in love with her, which was gifted to her by her mother. Krum forgot all his anger and started playing with the girl and making her comfortable. Swati fell unconscious and the other people protecting her were badly beaten up by Krum's men. He then took the girl in his hands and smiled.

Krum came in with a mindset of killing them, but his mind was blossomed and then he wanted to save the child and take her along with him. He was just about to leave when Shankar arrived in anger. He broke the door and threw it on Krum by turning it in a big and heavy size. Krum saw the door coming on him and screamed, "noooooo". He then threw the child in the hands of one of his men and ordered him to run away. Both Krum and his men were under the door and were finding it difficult to run away. However, the man with the baby managed to escape.

Shankar, ran towards Swati, saw her, but she was unconscious. Then he saw his child crying in a cradle but was surprised on seeing the second cradle empty. He thus asked Raman, "what happened? And why is this second cradle empty?"

Raman replied, "I am sorry, my friend. I tried my best to protect the twins."

Shankar said, "what? I had twins? Swati never mentioned about it."

Raman – "Yes, she wanted to surprise you, so she did not mention it."

Shankar was happy to know he had twins; a boy and a girl. He hugged Raman in pain and started crying on his shoulder for the loss. Shankar then asked, "In which direction did Krum's man run? Raman said, "I was facing towards the ground as I was beaten up, I never noticed them. Shankar then decided to take a risk by selecting a path and went in search of her daughter. However, it was too late and he was not able to find Krum's man.

On the other hand, the man suddenly stopped while running and breathing heavily turned back to see if he was being followed. He then sat on a bench; saw a man coming towards him. He was so exhausted that everything in front for him was blurred. A man came in front of him and asked to remember him.

Krum's man, in shock, replied, "who are you?"

"I am Grudge, you forgot me so soon?" He replied. "Remember that Diwali day, when you came drunk in my home?"

Krum's man replied in shock, "What? I killed you along with your family. How come you are still alive? And how did you find me?

"It is my lucky day. I saw you and started following you and waited for the right time," He answered. "Also, on that day, God showed mercy on me and kept me alive so that I could kill you and your child.

"What? Who? Hey, I am not married and this is not my child." Replied Krum's man.

Grudge replied, "I know you are a liar and I don't trust you." Grudge took the opportunity and stabbed the man directly in his heart. The man screamed, "Ahh Ahhhhh…" and fell on his feet. He then kicked him and went to attack the child with the knife in the air. At that moment, the crowd shouted, "catch the murderer." The man left Chiara and started running to save his life. The crowd noticed the man and started running to catch him. Amidst this, they left the infant behind. Krum's man slowly crawled towards Chiara and hid her under a lamp. He then slowly crawled a little away, so that no one could see Chiara and he died. Chiara was left alone in the corner of the street under the lamp crying.

Chapter 2

The story of Chiara

The time was passing and it was around 6 pm in the evening. Many vehicles passed by but no one was able to see the infant crying on the road as the street was too noisy. Chiara was getting restless and thus kept crying.

A drunken man came near the lamp and saw the infant. He muttered, “Oh my god, how can someone be so careless to leave her alone. My child, you are left alone and I too was once left alone.” As he went near Chiara to pick her up, he got blossomed and then took her along to his home.

Back in his colony, a fight was going on. Dhiraj’s gang was terribly beating a man who was asked to deliver some drugs to a man and hand over the money to their boss. Supposedly, he spent the money in whore & gambling and was now saying, “Stop hitting me! I was looted by a man who saw me taking money from the dealer.” Dhiraj stepped out of the car in style. He had a baseball bat with spikes on it. He walked towards the man and asked politely, “where is the money?" Before the man could answer, Dhiraj hit his head and tore it into two part, and the man collapsed. He hit the man before he could answer because he already found out that the money was spent in his casino only. This incident made everyone shiver out of fear. While walking in style towards his car, Dhiraj's eyes went on Chiara who was in the hands of the drunken man. He walked towards him and asked: "Hey, you drunken man. Who is this little girl and where did you find her?"

The man replied, "Mind your business. I found the girl and now I have decided to take care of her and raise her."

Dhiraj said, "You will take care of her. "Hahaha," he laughed and said, "look at yourself. First keep yourself tidy and then talk about raising a girl. I know you very well; you will raise her and once she grows up, you will sell her for your booze. Give the baby to me."

The drunken man replied, "And what are you going to do?"

"Shut up." Dhiraj slapped the man and then saw in the eyes of Chiara. At the very moment, Chiara blossomed her spell on the gangster. In the meantime, Dhiraj's men caught the drunken man and handed over Chiara to Dhiraj. They warned the drunken man and said, "Go home or you will not be alive." The drunken man was fully frightened and ran towards his home, crying. Dhiraj took Chiara in his car and went to a nearby store to buy her some clothes and infant formula.

As Swati regained consciousness, she saw Shankar sitting next to her. She was very happy and hugged him. However, when she saw everything messed up and her child missing, she started crying and was not able to control herself. Shankar went closer, comforted her and said, “Don’t worry, we will soon find her.” Swati, took the boy in her arms and again started crying for their loss. Shankar called Raman near him and said, “thank you for the support. If you were not there, nothing would have been possible.”

“Don’t talk nonsense. I am always on your side. Let me know if I can do anything for you,” replied Raman.

“No, my friend. You have done a lot and now we have decided to move to my brother's place and I will set up my office over there. You take care of yourself and inform me if you get to know anything about my daughter,” replied Shankar.

On that very day, Shankar along with Swati and Chirag moved to his brother’s place so that Krum could not find them and they could live peacefully. On the other hand, as Shankar threw the door on Krum and his men, Krum was badly injured and was taken to his home, but he went in a coma. His men died due to blood loss.

Chiara was so lucky for Dhiraj that from the very next day he started receiving good news regarding his businesses. Dhiraj was a gangster and had many illegal businesses and had many contacts because of which no one could stop him from getting anything in the city. He was unmarried and irrespective of the fact that he had all illegal businesses, he never had any bad habits. Slowly, Dhiraj started giving up all his bad businesses and concentrated only on two businesses which gave him good profits and that were Arms and Construction. Dhiraj decided to never get married because no woman would ever accept Chiara as her child.

After a few days, Shankar got an approval for a big project which benefited him a lot. Later, he decided to buy a house next to his brother's house so that they could live together. A few days passed and while recollecting some old memories, Swati remembered about the switch and thus said, "Shankar, I have put the switch in the bracelets and they are in the hands of both our children. And you know, our daughter has eyes similar to mine and the power to blossom anyone and make them fall in love with her."

"That's amazing," replied Shankar. "Don't worry, now or later, we will be able to identify our daughter with the bracelet she has."

Shankar then asked, "Did you give the dose which JOI asked you to give to our children at the time of birth so that they can get superpowers?"

"Yes," replied Swati. "I gave them the dose. The effect has already begun. Both are safe; the boy has fire in his eyes; no one would be able to stand in front of him once he is angry, he will turn into fire and his body will transform like stone."

"Are you kidding me? How are we going to control him?" asked Shankar.

"Don't worry, I will control him till he becomes an adult." Replied Swati.

They both happily smiled looking at each other.

A few years passed, Shankar daily tried searching for his daughter, hoping she was alive and safe, but he never got any information. One day, Shankar got a call from his old friend Vansh, who used to work with him.

"I've found your daughter. Pack your bags and come to the location I am sending."

"How do you know about it? And how are you so sure?" Shankar enquired.

"I called an acquaintance and he told me the story. Yesterday, I saw a girl who had eyes similar to Swati, so I thought to inform."

"Please let me know what can I offer to thank you?" replied Shankar.

"Are you mad? I don't want anything. All I want is your friendship. Come soon, I am waiting." Vansh said and hung up the call.

Shankar was a smart guy and sensed that something was wrong. He informed his wife and also said, "I don't trust this person. He is a bad person and can do anything to bring me down or kill me."

"Ok, you take care and keep me updated." Answered Swati.

Keeping in view his safety, he put a transmitter tooth in his mouth and also informed the local cops to keep an eye and record all movements.

Subsequently, Shankar packed his bags and left to reach the destination which was in the south. It was so far that it took him two days from the north. On his arrival, Vansh personally came to receive him.

Vansh had parked his car at the station and was waiting outside. Shankar saw Vansh and walked towards him. He then tapped his shoulder and said, "Hello, Vansh. How, are you?" Vansh, acted very happy to see him, hugged him and took his bag in his hands and said, "Hey, bro. It's so good to meet you. Let's go."

They both moved towards his car and planned to go to the hotel for lunch and then reach the destination. On the way, they spoke about many moments spent together and laughed merrily. Suddenly, Shankar remembered an old memory with Vansh. "Hey, do you remember the day when you were narrating the incident when you unknowingly fooled the boss, and unluckily the boss was standing behind and eavesdropped your narration?" asked Shankar.

"How can I forget that day? The boss fired me." Vansh answered.

"I remember how you angrily said, 'I will not leave you and spoil your future and went off," said Shankar.

Vansh simply smiled and ignored Shankar's words.

Albeit, Vansh later got a better post and got many promotions by doing hard work and finally reached the level which he never thought he could.

Present-day, Shankar was feeling sorry for that loss and kept asking for an apology. Shankar asked Vansh, "Did u forgive me?"

"Are you mad? I don't even think about the incident." Vansh assured.

Shankar was happy to know and said, "you have changed a lot."

Vansh gave a criminal smile and suddenly stopped the car. Shankar was surprised when he saw that Vansh had stopped the car in the middle of the jungle, where a scary house was built. There was an armed man and skeletons were hanging with name tags. Shankar realized that Vansh kept him so busy in talking that he did not notice the route Vansh drove to.

"This is Valco's Mansion," stated Vansh. "Where once a man comes with Vansh, does not go out alive."

"Who is Valco?" questioned Shankar.

"WELCOME TO HELL, brother," Vansh replied and laughed loudly. "A place where no one ever wants to come."

A number of men appeared near the car, pointing gun towards Shankar.

"Where is my daughter, Vansh?" questioned Shankar and caught Vansh's neck in anger.

Vansh said to his men, "Calm down boys" and to Shankar "Don't call me with that name." He pushed him away and his men caught Shankar. Vansh instructed his men to keep the guest in a special cell. He then went to his luxurious room, changed his clothes and took the avatar of Valco. After sometime, he went to Shankar and said, "I have already changed my name to Valco." He then narrated his past; all that happened after he was fired.

Swati was not able to track Shankar because Valco had a device installed a few kilometers before his residence which could defuse any transmitter, so that no one could find him. Swati was tensed and thus called her brother-in-law (Satish)

"Hello, Satish. Please come home. It's very urgent," said Swati.

"What happened? Why are you so tensed?" replied Satish.

"You please come home. I will explain everything to you in person," replied Swati.

Satish reached home and saw Swati on the sofa eagerly waiting for him. Swati saw Satish entering the house and went running to him. She told him about the situation.

"Oh my god. Wait, I will call my friend who is in the police. He will surely help us out," said Satish consolingly. He immediately called his friend and informed him about everything. With the help of his friend, they identified Shankar's location. Swati gave the details to the police and requested them to go to the location as soon as possible. Since the place was too far, the Police informed their south team and asked for help. Even after giving all the details and proof, the south team was not ready to help them and instead asked them to file F.I.R at the South police station. The

Officer in-charge of the South team went through the details and realized that he had seen the details of the location in a previous case too. He thus immediately forwarded the details to their tracking team and asked for an urgent report. The tracking team called back after sometime to report that the location was in a jungle and no resident, commercial or industrial land was sighted nearby. The officer took the radio in and gave the codes to the nearby patrolling team and asked them to have a visit, see the movement and report him at the earliest. The patrolling team reached the place and saw no one present there. As they moved a little forward, they sighted a gate. They reached the gate and were shocked to read 'Valco's mansion' written on the gate. They looked at each other in sheer terror and ran towards their car. They both where shivering so badly that they could not even open the car's door. Finally, they opened the door and immediately took the radio in hand to inform the officer.

"Sir," said the policeman.

At the very moment, a man from Valco's mansion was outside, who went to buy something. He saw two police personnel trying to inform someone about the place.

Before they could inform anything further to the Officer, the man immediately stabbed both the police personnel with a knife. One of the policemen, in pain tried to get up and caught the man. He took the knife and stabbed him in his heart. The other policeman was severely injured and left unconscious on the ground.

"What happened? Reply to me," The Officer in-charge on the other side of radio questioned in shock. "Anyone there? What did you see? Why are you not speaking?"

The wounded policeman took the radio in his hand and said only one thing, **"VALCO'S MANSION."** He then covered the dead body of the man with leaves and carried his friend slowly to his car. He then went to the driving seat and left for the hospital, both of them were safe. The main Officer in-charge, after hearing the name sat on the chair in shock and shouted, "team, gather in my office, right now." He also called the north police team.

"How do you know Valco?" He questioned.

North team replied, "Who Valco? We gave you details of a missing person named Shankar."

"The person is in a grave danger. Once anyone enters that valley, he does not come back. We have been searching for that place for many years, but have never found such a place," said the Officer in-charge. "We are very happy for the details you've shared and are ready to take a call on Valco."

The south police team called all their seniors and explained the situation. The seniors were happy for the progress and completed all the paper work and instructed the team to bring Valco; either dead or alive. The South police team then called the army to help them catch the culprit. All police personnel and army were suited up with all maximum gears possible and went in search of Valco.

When the team reached the spot, all the men started moving towards the main gate. However, the lead officer noticed the route was splitting. He then split the team in two and instructed everyone to cover the whole place and further split the team whenever they felt the need. With this approach, they found all the exit points and appointed five teams. The team split in five directions. Each team had ten commandos and a sniper to back them up.

Two members of the first team fell in a trap by pressing the wrong button while they were trying to open the gate. They fell in a pond, where two giant alligators were hungrily waiting for food. Luckily, the two commandos who fell were highly trained and managed to kill the alligators. However, they were trapped in the pond and waited for their teammates to save them. The other commandoes escaped the trap and tried the other way to enter the mansion. The other four teams managed to enter the mansion from each direction. Valco's security was watching everything and informed Valco about it.

The attack started by the commandos and the sniper played a very important role by killing all the men securing from top bunkers. Valco's 75% unit was destroyed and he had no option other than surrendering himself to the police. The police had so many questions for Valco and therefore they wanted him alive. So, they decided not kill him. Valco knew many secrets; whom and what he was dealing in. The army went in search of Shankar. The team found a few people and took them to the hospital in their jeep. The Police saved the two commandos who fell in the pond and asked to search for Shankar. The main officer in-charge saw a man and identified him as Shankar with the help of the photo given by the North team. As he saw Shankar, he muttered, “how could anyone be so cruel to torture a man so badly,” The officer presumed Shankar to be dead. However, to his surprise, when he checked his wrist, he could feel the pulse. Shankar was unconscious and thus the Officer immediately carried him on his shoulder and rushed to the hospital.

After sometime, the doctors informed the Officer that Shankar was in a critical condition and their team was working hard to bring him in a normal condition.

“If you would have been a minute late, he would have not been alive. Who is this man? His back is cut with a sharp knife, his backbone is visible, his left leg bone is fractured, the right-hand bone is fractured and two fingers are cut. His arms and body are so stiff, it appears that he is some highly trained person because any normal man would have died on the spot, but he is very strong. I am really surprised to see a person like him.”

“We don’t know his personal information, doctor. He is from the north and we will inform his family and they will be here soon,” said the Officer.

The Officer in-charge called the North police team and informed them about Shankar.

“You need to rush here. He is in a critical condition,” the Officer informed the north police team.

Satish received the news through his friend and was in utter shock.

"What did the police say? Why are you not speaking anything?" Swati questioned.

"They've found Shankar, but he is in a critical condition. I need to go there immediately," replied Satish, crying.

"No, what are you saying? This is not possible. Wait, I am also coming with you," replied Swati.

"No, you cannot come along. I will handle the situation. You take care of Chirag and don't tell him anything."

Swati thought about Chirag and thus agreed. "Ok, you go and keep me updated," said Swati in a low voice.

Chapter 3

The superpowers

Chirag stood behind eavesdropping the conversation between Swati and Satish. As he saw his mom crying after hearing about his dad, he entered the room and started staring at his mom with anger filled eyes. He became so angry that his body turned hot as fire. His mom and uncle were shocked seeing him burning like fire.

"Chirag, my son, clam down. Your anger will set the house on fire," said Swati, but Chirag was not in a mood to listen.

"Look here, I am your mom, I will explain you everything," said Swati. Chirag looked in Swati's eyes and was blossomed. His temperature reduced. His uncle brought a towel and covered him immediately. He then explained him everything and asked him to keep calm and not to do anything stupid which could end their lives. Chirag was a very intelligent boy who understood the situation and then controlled his powers.

"How come I have this power?" questioned Chirag.

"My son, it is not the right time to talk about it," answered Swati. She then made Chirag promise that he would never mention about the power to anyone and also not to use it.

Satish packed his bags, booked air tickets and left for the South. He reached there and directly went to the hospital, met Shankar and sat near him. The officer came to Satish and enquired about Shankar. Satish then told everything about Shankar to the Officer.

"We are proud to have heroes like Shankar," said the Officer smilingly. "I will clear all the formalities. You take care of him," he said and left for the station.

The doctor entered the room and informed that Shankar is out of danger and will be discharged in a week. Satish called Swati and informed her about everything. Swati was happy after hearing the news and was eagerly waiting to see Shankar.

Valco was given fourteen years of imprisonment as only a few crimes were proven, and thus was saved from life imprisonment. He was taken to afar prison, somewhere in the middle of the sea, where all the blackest criminals were imprisoned.

Back at Dhiraj's place, Chiara was growing very cheerful and naughty. She used her charm on Dhiraj and took all the luxurious things she wanted. She was named Minnie by Dhiraj because his younger sister was also named Minnie and he loved her a lot. But unfortunately, Dhiraj was thrown out of his house for his behaviors and after that, he never saw his family.

One day, Dhiraj was very frustrated as he missed a million-dollar deal because of the carelessness of his employs. On the very same day, Minnie's school principal called Dhiraj and informed him about the involvement of Minnie in a fight and she had beaten up a girl so badly that the girl was hospitalized. Dhiraj went to the school and saw Minnie fully messed up; her shirt was torn and she had scratch marks on her hands. He then ran towards Minnie and asked, "What happened? Who did this to you?"

"Papa, that girl started the fight. She teased me and touched me in a vulgar manner," replied Minnie.

Dhiraj angrily got up and started shouting at the teacher.

"Is this what happens in your school? Look at her condition. What are you teachers paid salary for if you are not able to take care of children?"

"Sir, your daughter is the reason that one of our students is in the hospital and you are still supporting your daughter? You cannot blame us for your daughter's mistake, we are paid to teach and not babysit the students," replied the teacher.

"According to me, Minnie has done a good job by sending her to the hospital," claimed Dhiraj.

"Like father, like daughter. Go to the principal and talk to her regarding this. I don't want to talk to you."

"Even I am not interested in talking to you," said Dhiraj arrogantly and moved towards the principal's office. He entered the room and started shouting at the principal, "Is this what you people teach the students; how to get vulgar in class?"

"Mister, do you know whom are you taking to? This is my office and not your play arena that you can enter anytime you wish too," replied the principal firmly.

"Oh! So, do you know whom you are talking to? Kindly call your trusty and tell him who has come to your office and then give the phone to me."

"Why do I need to get frightened? I won't call anyone. Are you trying to scare me?" said the principal.

Dhiraj took his phone out from his pocket and dialed the school trusty.

"I don't want this guy to be the principal and you better change the teaching staff, they are so rude to me."

"Ok, Noted," replied the trusty and kept the call."

"TRING TRING," said Dhiraj, staring at the principal.

Principal's phone rang immediately. "Who are you?" Asked the principal shockingly.

"Your GODFATHER," replied Dhiraj in style.

The principal picked up the call. "YOU ARE FIRED," said the person on call.

"Never mess with people you don't know. The next time I see you anywhere, you are…" said Dhiraj making an action with his hand, "FINISH."

When Dhiraj was leaving, the teacher who argued with him stood joining hands in front of him. She kept asking for an apology.

"Please don't take away my job, I am sorry," pleaded the teacher.

"Once I speak something, its similar to a permanent scratch on a wall; can neither be rubbed nor altered," replied Dhiraj cruelly. Dhiraj held Minnie's hand, went towards the car and drove her home.

He then accompanied Minnie to her room and asked her to freshen up. He waited for her to return and checked her books in the meantime. As Minnie returned, Dhiraj made her sit in front of him.

"Listen carefully, Minnie." Said Dhiraj in an asserting tone.

Minnie nodded.

"My father once taught me that we should never let our child down in front of anyone. If we do so, the next time, our child will not be able to face that person and that person will always tease him. Instead, we should support him and close the matter then and there. However, later when we get home, we must make them understand and realize their mistake, so that they don't repeat it. Therefore, I didn't scold you there. However, Minnie, you need to realize that it was your mistake too," explained Dhiraj.

That day, Dhiraj didn't look in her eyes because he knew if he did so, he would forget everything and allow her to play. Minnie was very upset and felt that she was invisible for Dhiraj as he scolded her. When Dhiraj turned back to hold Minnie, he was shocked as Minnie was missing. Dhiraj ran towards the window and saw down. To his surprise, no one was there. Dhiraj got emotional and called all his men and asked them to search for Minnie. Dhiraj left the room and started searching for Minnie, but she was found nowhere.

In reality, Minnie was in the room, standing on the same position. She never moved an inch and stood with her head down. However, when Dhiraj went near the window, Minnie looked up and was confused seeing Dhiraj searching for her whilst she was standing right in front of him. Minnie was shocked and started jumping in excitement. She was so happy that she did not know how to get back to normal. However, she managed to control her emotions and her mind by closing her eyes. She then turned normal and went to Dhiraj asking for forgiveness. Dhiraj was shocked to see Minnie coming out from her room.

"Where did you go, Minnie?" Questioned Dhiraj.

"I didn't go anywhere. It was you who got tensed and left the room," replied Minnie innocently.

"Did you again use your charm on me?" Questioned Dhiraj.

"No, I didn't do anything," replied Minnie laughingly and went into the room. At the same time, Dhiraj got a call from his employ informing that a deal was fixed. Dhiraj thus got diverted and completely forgot about Minnie.

Minnie started using her invisibility power from the age of just twelve. She used to get invisible and wandered on the roads at night. She went to parks, playgrounds and even scared people by touching them. Sometimes, she used to go near people and laugh loudly, so that they get scared and run away.

One day, she went to her friend's place to check what she was doing. She reached there around 11 pm and rang the doorbell. Her friend's father opened the door and looked out. In the meantime, Minnie silently entered and ran towards her friend. Her friend's father was shocked to see the entrance empty and said, "it might be some naughty kid." He then locked the door and went to his bedroom. Minnie saw her friend lying on the bed and reading some novel. Minnie then pulled her legs and laughed loudly. Her friend got afraid, threw the book and went running to her father. Minnie then read the novel a little and left for her home through the main door. Due to her negligence, she left the door open. She then reached her home and slept off.

The next day, when Minnie went to school, she met the same friend.

"Hi, how are you?" questioned Minnie.

"Hi, I am good. Thank you," replied her friend in a low voice.

"I was planning to read a novel lately. Can you suggest me a good one?" Asked Minnie.

"I don't read novels," replied her friend hesitatingly. She lied as she thought if she agreed, Minnie would ask for her Novel. "Do you know, last night someone entered my house and robbed my dad's precious watch which was gifted by his boss. It was very costly."

"Oh, that's bad news," said Minnie and then smirked. She thought to herself that she was the one who left the door open last night.

Amidst all this, Minnie couldn't sleep properly at times; she used to feel the emotions of missing someone, but never knew who she was missing. She only felt an attachment and felt as if someone was talking about her. On the other hand, his brother Chirag experienced the same.

Chapter 4

Dreams

Minnie and Chirag, from a very young age, used to get dreams about each other, yet they didn't know who the other person was. Minnie used to get dreams about Chirag sitting, playing with his friends, going to school, spending time with his parents, and also crying at times. When Minnie saw Chirag laughing, then her entire day used to be exciting. On the contrary, when she saw Chirag crying in her dreams, then she used to be sad the entire day. Albeit she used to ignore the dreams, she couldn't figure out why they affected her so much. Chirag, on the other hand, experienced the same. The twins were connected internally and thus they used to see each other in their dreams. Unaware of this fact, they continued living their lives.

Years passed, Chirag grew up as a very handsome boy, such that he could attract any girl with his charm. He was in the final year of completing his education and was about to become a scientist. On his 21st birthday, his mom and dad took him to the same place where he was born. They explained him the entire story and then celebrated his birthday together. After reaching home, the next day, Swati asked Chirag to come to her room.

"Yes, maa. You called," said Chirag politely.

"I want to tell you something. We decided not to tell you, but I believe it is the right time to tell the same," replied Swati.

"Yes maa. Please, tell me," asked Chirag.

"I delivered twins," replied Swati in a low voice.

"What?" Replied Chirag in utter shock. "Where is he now and why is he not staying with us?"

"You have a sister. We named her Chiara. We lost her in an act of revenge and she is still missing," explained Swati.

"Oh no, I wish she was with me. I always wanted a sister." Replied Chirag in a deep voice.

"Don't worry, Chirag. We shall soon find her."

"Yes maa, definitely. But how am I supposed to identify her if she ever meets me?"

"Good question, Chirag. You can identify her easily. She has the power to blossom anyone with her charm. She also has invisibility power and eyes similar to mine. She has the same bracelet as you do," explained Swati.

"I will find her and definitely bring her back; we will soon have a reunion," said Chirag positively.

"If you join both your bracelets, you will see a unique symbol of a star with a message, 'Time and Tide Wait for None'. Your dad has been trying to find her, but she is still missing. I really hope we find her before I die," said Swati with tears in her eyes.

Chirag hugged his mom and consoled her. He then went to his dad and said, "Don't worry, Papa. We will soon find Chiara and unite again."

"Okay, so your mom told everything to you?" questioned Shankar with a smile. Chirag then hugged him and said, "thank you for everything."

As Chirag was moving towards his room, Swati stopped him.

"Hey, Chirag. I take back the promise which I compelled you to make as a kid. Now, you definitely can use your power but make sure you do it wisely so that no innocent is hurt. Never let anyone know the truth about this power," said Swati and then gifted him a fire suit." Chirag happily accepted the suit and decided to get trained.

Minnie on other hand grew very charming, and looked a little like her mother. She was so smart as if she was gifted all the intelligence. She completed her education in nuclear studies and joined in the construction business with Dhiraj. She worked like a professional and became his right hand. Meanwhile, she controlled her powers but never told anyone about it; not even Dhiraj.

One night, MI-CHI (Minnie and Chirag) both had a similar dream and saw each other.

Chirag: The dream was set in a mall, where Chirag entered first with his friends, laughing and enjoying. Suddenly, Chirag stopped and felt Goosebumps and experienced a feeling of attachment, as if there was someone he knew, but couldn't figure out. He turned back and observed all the strangers closely but felt clueless. He ignored everything and walked ahead. As he suddenly turned back to his friend, someone crossed him and at the very moment a strange thunder was heard.

Minnie: Her dream was set in the same mall, where she entered alone for purchasing a gift for Dhiraj. As soon as she entered, she felt Goosebumps and experienced a feeling of attachment, as if there was someone she knew, but couldn't figure out. She kept walking and then a strange thunder was heard. She looked at the boy next to her and realized that she has some connection with him.

Chirag and Minnie, both felt a connect on seeing each other.

Back in reality, a sudden thunder was heard and both MI-CHI woke up at the same time. They stepped out from their beds and saw the time, it was 5:00 am. They both were sweating. The interesting part was that Minnie went invisible when she woke up and Chirag was about to burn his bed. They both relaxed and then turned normal.

Chirag ignored the dream, drank some water and slept off. However, Minnie wasn't able to figure out as how she became invisible even after possessing the complete control of it. She tried recognizing the face she saw last, but was not able to do so. She spent almost two hours thinking about it, but failing to recognize the face, she muttered, "what a crap, man" and slept off again.

After a month, Minnie wore the same dress which she wore in her dream and was planning to visit her friend and then go for a meeting scheduled by Dhiraj with his international clients. Minnie drove to her friend's place but noticed that her house was locked. She called her friend and found that her friend was out of town on a trip with her family. Minnie hit on her steering and thought she should've called her friend beforehand. She then started to check her phone in order to pass the time before her meeting. A message popped from a shopping site stating, 'Celebrating our 25th anniversary, visit our store till 19th March and grab the best outfits with flat 25% off. She then checked the date and it was 19th March. She felt happy and searched for nearby malls which had their store and decided to visit the Life Line mall as it was just 11am and the meeting was scheduled at 3pm. She also realized that it was Dhiraj's birthday and thus decided to buy a good gift and surprise him. She started driving to reach the mall which was 2km away, but was stuck in a traffic jam.

On the other hand, Chirag was ready to go on an outing with his friends. His friend picked him up from home to reach at their friend's place. As soon as they reached there, they found that he was not home. Chirag asked his parents and they informed him that his friend went to Life Line mall for picking up a food parcel which they planned for their outing. They decided to wait for their friend to come home and then leave for the outing.

It was more than half an hour waiting and Chirag thus called his friend and scolded him for the delay.

The friend replied, "The shop is closed and the owner says he is on the way and will reach in 5 minutes."

Chirag decided to go to the mall and then go for outing directly from there.

Chirag entered first with his friends, laughing and enjoying. After a few minutes, Minnie entered the mall alone for purchasing a gift for Dhiraj. Suddenly, Chirag stopped and felt Goosebumps and experienced a feeling of attachment, as if there was someone he knew, but couldn't figure out. He turned back and observed all the strangers closely but felt clueless. He ignored everything and walked ahead. As he suddenly turned back to his friend, Minnie crossed him and at the very moment a strange thunder was heard. Both Chirag and Minnie were shocked. However, the very next moment, they ignored each other and went away.

Minnie purchased a nice watch and left for home. She decided to give the watch to Dhiraj after the meeting. On the other hand, Chirag scolded the shop owner for his irresponsible behavior, took his food parcel and continued for their outing.

To their great misfortune, the car got punctured on the way. The boys got down and fixed the puncture. However, after driving for half an hour, another tire was punctured because all 4 tiers were in worst condition and not maintained. Chirag, in anger, banged the dash board and then got down angrily. He started scolding his friend for his irresponsible behavior and both friends had a heated argument. Later, one of the boys went to search for a tire shop and Chirag in anger walked away.

"Pick me up when all the tires are fixed and do not call me before that," said Chirag angrily.

All his friends were afraid of his anger and they knew that if he is not in a good mood, he is better to be left alone and not mess up with. Chirag walked 1km away and he then sensed something bad was going to happen. He looked straight far sighting two heavy loaded lorries with metal balls, one overtaking the other in full speed were going to collide with a school bus which was coming from the opposite direction. The school bus was blowing horn continuously, but the lorries were not ready to stop. Chirag had his suit ready, but the problem was he would get lighted up only when he was in an angry mood. He decided and that was the moment Chirag lighted himself and flew to that place. He blew both the front tires of the lorries with fireballs and they fell on another side of the road and thus the school bus got the way and was saved from an accident. Chirag flew away immediately after the incident and started walking back normally towards his friends. One of the lorries fell safely on sand where all metal balls rolled over the sand, but one ball which was on the top, opened. The crowd was stunned seeing guns on one side and explosive powder on the other side in the metal ball. The other lorry managed to escape from the spot. Chirag covered his face with his handkerchief and silently managed to climb on the other lorry. Police rushed on the spot and arrested the driver for drink and drive case and for carrying explosives.

Chirag then reached the destination where the lorry was heading to and was shocked at seeing the place. The place was very huge; at one side a lab was built, on the other side men were being trained and there was a big warehouse in the corner. It was fully safeguarded by commandoes everywhere with fully armed weapons. Chirag took many photos of the location. When he was trying to escape, a guy caught him from back and was about to shout. However, Chirag used his technical fighting style and held the neck of the guard so tightly that he wasn't able to shout. Chirag then made him unconscious by hitting him on the head and managed to escape. The camera recorded every moment of Chirag. Amidst all this, he got lucky that no one was able to see his face.

Chirag reached home and showed everything to his parents

"It was a dangerous act," said Shankar, closing the file in hand. "Forget everything; as if nothing happened." Shankar smiled reassuringly. "It would be a military camp and you would have mistaken it as a wrong place." Shankar said so because he did not want to lose his son and thus ended the conversation.

In the meantime, Minnie was attending the meeting with the international clients along with Dhiraj. They were discussing about the new idea of bringing drugs and guns in-country and the supply chain for the same. Many other big dealers across the Globe were present in that meeting.

Chapter 5

Shadow

In a tea break, Dhiraj met Shadow who was from London. He was the topmost dangerous dealers who never gave up in his life and when we talk about brain, no one could compete him in making things which were never possible to even think of. The glasses which he wore were not normal; the lenses scanned every object which passed near his eyes, showing him what a person was hiding, the temperature of the person and even judged his next move. The temples of the eyeglasses were especially made with a device fitted in, which helped him to hear anything as clear as crystal. For example, even a thin air that passes by could be heard. The glasses were called the 'Eagle's Eye'.

Next, he had a watch which didn't show time, rather it displayed every other possible feature, like, what is the pulse rate, the next task to be done, had a voice command to type anything and send it to anyone, vibrated when it was time for medicine and activated any weapon needed over voice command which then reached him within a fraction of seconds.

The next was the buttons on his coat; they were not normal buttons; those were activated with the watch and once commanded the target gets locked and the buttons turn into small and dangerous bombs which can explode anyone in parts.

Before any meeting, Shadow took around one hour to set up everything with the watch and then moved out. He was thus called Shadow, the unstoppable.

Dhiraj’s main motive of attending the meeting was to meet Shadow because he was interested to make a big deal that was to make an unstoppable and powerful villain. Shadow knew that this was not possible without Minnie’s mind as she was a nuclear expert. Both agreed to the deal but the international deal did not go through because Dhiraj did not find profit in that deal. Minnie was not happy because the deal was not cracked.

While going back home, Minnie tapped Dhiraj's shoulder and asked, "Are you sad for not getting the deal?"

“No, not at all. This deal was just a time pass," said Dhiraj reassuringly.

“Hmmm... Ok. Happy birthday, dad," said Minnie with a bright smile and then gifted him the watch. Dhiraj took the watch and said, "thank you." He opened the cover and saw it was just like what he wanted.

“It is as beautiful as you. I will always wear this so that whenever I see it, I will get reminded of you."

"So sweet. Where is the party?" questioned Minnie and laughed happily.

“Let us go to your favorite restaurant and have dinner together, what say?" asked Dhiraj.

“Ok, dad. Love you." replied Minnie in excitement.

“I Love you too, my naughty daughter,” replied Dhiraj. He then dropped Minnie home and asked her to get ready. “I have got a work to complete. Get ready before I come back,” said Dhiraj and left for the warehouse.

Since he got the information about the truck incident, he wanted to clear the matter as soon as possible. The matter with the police was already settled after the lorry was identified to be of Dhiraj. As he reached the warehouse, he checked the camera and felt troubled when he saw that a boy took the photos of the location. Thus, he decided not to waste time any further and clear the whole stuff and shift it to another warehouse because he knew the boy would come finding for him. Dhiraj called both the truck drivers and the man who was beaten up by Chirag and asked them only one question, “how did that boy manage to enter this property?” The question was never answered because all the three men were scared as it was the biggest mistake which costed Dhiraj a lot. Dhiraj instructed his men to clear the stuff and went off. The men followed his instruction and even murdered the people who they kidnapped and kept as slaves.

On the other hand, Chirag went to his room and sat thinking about the worst day he had today. He tried recollecting everything that happened. Suddenly, a moment clicked when he saw a girl today and he could relate that incident seen a month back in his dream as well. Chirag was shocked and asked himself, "why? Why did it happen? How come an event in the dream became a reality?" Chirag was trying to recollect the girl's face in the dream and the one he saw today, but unfortunately was not able to recognize it. The same thing was going on with Minnie; she too also was not able to recognize the boy.

Dhiraj reached home and kept thinking about the incident that happened. He then dressed up to go out for a dinner with Minnie. After a few hours, Dhiraj and Minnie returned home and were happy that they had a great time together.

"Minnie, I will freshen up and come to meet you. I need to talk," said Dhiraj walking towards him room.

"Sure, dad." Said Minnie.

Subsequently, Minnie went to her room and while she was taking rest, she heard a knock. Dhiraj stepped in and informed Minnie about the incident which took place and asked her to take care of it and then went away. Minnie called in the office and asked them to send the clip so that she could see if the boy had left any clue behind. As she received the video, she fully focused on it and observed that the boy was wearing a safe suit which was clearly seen. She decided to go in the morning to find the suit. Then she went to bed thinking about the day which went so bad and slowly closed her eyes and slept off. At the same time, Chirag also slept off and they both entered the dream world.

Minnie: She was in a party and the ambience was very noisy and fully dark. She was standing near the bar counter and saw a boy entering the club with his friends. She saw him coming towards her with his friends to grab a drink. She heard the boy asking the bartender for four shots.

Chirag: He entered a bar with his friends and noticed a girl standing near the bar counter. His friends planned to have a drink and then go to the dance floor. Chirag agreed and went near the bar counter. He saw Minnie with a few girls and reached near the counter. Turning towards the bartender, he shouted, "Hey man, give me four shots, please." He then took the shots and went to the dance floor with his friends.

Both Minnie and Chirag got up again from the dream, but this time both remembered the face of each other. They both felt clueless and went back to sleep.

The next day, Minnie got ready and called her man enquiring about any person who could stitch a suit which can be used for a superpower role. Her source gave her a list of ten people who stitched attires for the film industry. Minnie reached all the ten stores one by one and showed them the suit which the boy wore, but unfortunately no one had stitched anything like that. When Minnie reached the last store, the tailor said, "the suit which you are looking for cannot be found in this city or even in this country. It is only made abroad or the person would have brought the material home and could have done the stitching."

"Ok, thank you for the information," replied Minnie disappointedly. She then got frustrated, went towards the car and left the place.

Chirag went back to the place where he saw the truck. This time he went with an intention to get more details on the activities undertaken there. When he reached the place, he was stunned seeing the land empty and thought to himself, "where the hell is everyone." He looked at the photos and then again looked towards the spot. He doubted whether he was at the exact location or not. As he walked back towards the road, he saw a car arriving at the spot. As the car stopped, a few men with arms stepped out of the car and moved towards the spot talking about the incident that happened. Chirag, casually walked and went to them.

"Hey, man. Are you guys from military?" questioned Chirag.

"No. Who are you and why have you come here?" replied the man.

"I am a property broker and sell lands. I saw this property and thus have come here to enquire if this is for sale," questioned Chirag.

"No, it's not for sale. We are here to safeguard this place so that we can reply to people like you," replied the man and laughed.

"Ok, chill man. That's what I was thinking that a dumb like you cannot be in the army."

“Hey, man. Hold your tongue and leave the place before I shoot you on your head. You have no idea whose place it is.” Warned the man.

“Ok, calm down. By the way, tell me whose property is it, so that I can ask him directly if he is interested to sell.”

“Are you mad or what? I told you the property is not for sale, so better just leave before my temper bursts and I kill you.” Replied the man angrily.

Chirag pretended to leave the place but kept waiting for the guards to leave so that he could follow them. Chirag found out that it was Dhiraj’s home where the guards went at last. Standing outside the villa, Chirag saw Minnie in the balcony. She was facing backside so he was not able to see her face and thus left the place and went home. Chirag was confused and had no idea about what to do so he told his dad, “I went to that place but found nothing; the place was empty.”

“Empty? I told you to stay out of it and that it’s not your job to handle, why don’t you listen to me? I have lost my daughter and now I am not in a state to lose you. Why don’t you understand?” replied Shankar angrily.

“Dad, I always listen to you. However, here, I felt that something is fishy and so I went; I have been given powers not to sit at home and ignore the situation. I am a grown man and I can handle the situation. I just came to inform you because I did not want to do anything without informing you,” said Chirag in a low voice.

“Oh, ok. Come here.” Said Shankar and hugged him. “Days passed and now you are a grown up. I taught you right and wrong when you were small, but now you have the idea to judge the situation. Don’t get caught, do whatever you want to do but do it with proper planning and save the world. I am proud of you, my son.”

“Thank you, dad,” said Chirag and took the blessings of Shankar. As he was leaving the room, Shankar said from behind, “Chirag, yesterday when you told about it, I already knew that you have got a hunch and that is very dangerous for our planet, so take steps carefully and if you need support, I am always there for you.”

Chirag went into his working lab and started to draw a structure. He was trying to figure out the way to catch the gangsters.

Chapter 6

Mother of Hope

25th March

It was Minnie's friend's birthday and they had a small celebration in the afternoon with a cake cutting. They then went to the ashram to gift new dresses to all the children and spent some time there. Her friend then asked all her friends to go back home, get ready and meet at the dinner party organized by her.

"Sorry, babes. I will not be able to come as I have a meeting with Dad regarding some work," said Minnie.

"Now don't be so workaholic. We know only your dad is everything for you, but my birthday comes once in a year, so stop acting and join us or I will not talk to you." Said her friend.

"Don't be a drama queen," said Minnie. "I will try to come."

Minnie went home and spoke to Dhiraj about the dinner party.

"Ok, you go ahead. I will make the plan and mail it to you, you may check it later and inform me if you feel any change is required," said Dhiraj happily.

"Thank you, Dad. I love you." Minnie hugged Dhiraj and ran towards her room to get dressed up. After half an hour, she was ready and started walking to move out.

"OMG, someone's looking very adorable today. Please don't kill anyone with your looks," said Dhiraj.

"Stop it, Dad," said Minnie smilingly.

"Are you going to a dinner party or on a date with a guy, huh?" questioned Dhiraj raising his eyebrows.

"I don't like to go on date and there is no guy born to be so lucky to have me," said Minnie and laughed.

"Ok, sweetheart. Now go and enjoy the party. If you happen to get late, inform me beforehand." Replied Dhiraj.

"Sure, dad." Said Minnie and left for the party.

Minnie reached the restaurant and had fun with all her friends. They then decided to extend the party and visit a new Disco which was recently inaugurated called Ola's club and then go home later.

"Whoa girls, I told you I'd come only for the dinner and now you are taking full benefits of my freedom. You guys know that I hate loud music and feel uncomfortable in Disco." Said Minnie.

"Come on, Minnie. I promise we will leave soon. We will surely have fun. Let's go, please." Requested her friend.

Minnie agreed and they all left for the disco.

On the other hand, Chirag received a message on his friends' group. "Hey, punks. What are your plans for today?"

Chirag saw the message and replied that he was busy. All other friends decided to visit a new Disco which was recently inaugurated called Ola's Club. Chirag's friends later decided to give him a surprise and pick him up from his place. All his friends got ready and reached his home.

"Hi, Uncle. Where is Chirag?" his friend questioned.

"Wait a minute," replied Shankar smilingly. "Well, everyone's looking great. Where are you heading to?"

"Nothing special, uncle. We all just decided to take a break and so thought to spend some time together." Answered Chirag's friend.

"Ok, then enjoy. Also, you people better know where Chirag would be right now. Go meet him and take him along." Said Shankar. "However, if you get late at night, let me know beforehand."

"Sure, uncle," replied the boy.

All the boys together went to Chirag's workplace and surprised him.

"Surprise," exclaimed the boys. "Hey, boy. What are you up to?" questioned one of his friends.

"Seriously, what are you guys doing here? At least knock the door before you enter, guys." Replied Chirag.

"Knock the door? Now what is that? We will enter as we wish to and now stop being a nerd and get up. We have already spoken to your dad and you are coming with us right away. And that's an order and not a request." Said his friend and all laughed.

"Shut up, I'm up to something and thus cannot come. You guys carry on." Replied Chirag.

"What are you up to?" questioned his friend.

"Please, don't interfere. You guys go ahead. We'll go out some other day." Requested Chirag.

"You better leave all this or we all will sit here and no one will move out without you. If you are not coming, then we will also not go." Replied his friend adamantly.

"Uhh. What a drama, guys. Fine, you all wait in the car and I will join you in ten minutes." Said Chirag.

"Now that's the spirit." Said his friend and they all moved out. Chirag then left his work undone and went to his room to get ready. After sometime, he joined his friends and they all left for Disco.

Shankar and Swati were sitting alone in the hall.

"Hey, listen. I got something for us." Exclaimed Shankar.

"For us? What do you mean, 'us'?" asked Swati.

Shankar went in the lab and came out with a painting. He then opened the cover and showed her the paining.

"It's called, 'Mother of hope.' How is it?" questioned Shankar.

"Wow, it's so beautiful. What an art! But why did you suddenly buy a painting?" Asked Swati.

"A few days back Raman called me and mentioned about a lady who according to him has solved many of his family and business-related problems. The lady has warned him of his future related problems as well. Raman very confidently said that the lady can read the past of any person and he has experienced it personally. He thus asked me to visit the lady and ask about our daughter Chiara.

In the initial, I didn't show interest, but later I decided to meet the lady once. I was shocked on seeing the ambience as it was a dark room and a square shape was drawn on the ground. All the walls were having something written in Sanskrit, probably mantras. When I entered the second room, I saw the lady sitting and chanting some mantras. Suddenly, she stopped and turned around. She started staring me and asked me to sit and questioned, 'How was your journey to the south? You had fun?'

I was shocked and thus asked her of how she knew all that. She answered that she knew everything as she had powers to see anyone's past and futuristic events. I then asked her about my daughter. She told me to visit her the next day and that she will give a painting.

The next day, she gave me this painting asked me to hang this in my room facing south-east direction and worship it every Thursday by meditating and facing the painting. This should be done for four months and then we will surely get the results before or after completing the task. So, I decided to buy the painting and as Chirag was not home therefore, I thought to show this to you and ask for permission to hang this in our room."

Swati was completely clueless and then suddenly started laughing at Shankar. "How do you manage to believe in things which are hoax?"

"Let's try this. What's wrong in trying?" replied Shankar, scratching his head.

"If you want to try this, then go ahead and hang the painting, but remember, I don't trust all this stupidity. You may surely meditate, but I will pray to god and not worship any hoax."

"Ok, dear. I will do anything to get my daughter. I will not force you." Replied Shankar smilingly.

(Mother of Hope)

In the meantime, Chirag and his friends reached the Disco. The parking was completely full and the place was very crowded. Finally, they got a parking and got down adjusting their dresses and then everyone moved towards the entrance. The guard stopped them and said, “No bachelor boys allowed, only couple entry.”

“I told you I don’t want to join. You guys never listen to me.” Said Chirag.

“Shut up, let me talk to him.” Asserted his friend.

“Move aside. Give place to others to enter.” Instructed the guard.

“Hey, boss. Who said we are bachelors? Our Girls are waiting near the car; you give us the pass. They will join us now.” Said Chirag’s friend.

"Come as a couple and I will allow you. I have seen many like you.” Replied the guard.

As they all were moving down, they saw a group of five girls moving towards the entrance of the Disco. One of Chirag’s friend said, “Wait guys, look there. These girls can help us go inside. I will go and talk to them. Till then you guys wait here.” He then grabbed Chirag’s hand and took him along so that the girls would agree; as Chirag was charming and good looking.

As they went near the girls, Chirag’s friend said, “Hey, beautiful. I think you girls are going to bring down the disk as you all look so gorgeous.”

“Excuse me?” replied one of the girls.

“Ok, I will come to the point. He is my friend Chirag and he is leaving us tomorrow and going abroad, so we wanted to party before he leaves. Can you girls help us in getting the entry passes and in return we shall buy you drinks?” asked his friend.

"Oh, really," replied the girl.

Chirag nodded with a mixed reaction.

"Ok, let's go. But once we get inside, we don't know you and you don't know us. Is it ok?"

"Superb, thank you." Said Chirag's friend smilingly. He then waved at his other friends and asked them to join. As they came near, he said, "let's rock and roll, guys."

They all then moved towards the entrance. The Guard stopped them again and asked, "you guys again?"

"Are they really with you?" questioned the guard looking at the girls.

"We are not what you think. See, we are in couples." Said Chirag's friend.

"Ok, get inside. But my eyes will be on you."

Chirag entered the club with his friends. Chirag's friend said, "let's have a drink and then go to the dance floor." Chirag said, "ok Bro" and went towards the bar counter. Minnie saw him coming towards her with his friends to grab a drink. Chirag also saw Minnie with a few girls. He reached near the bar counter. They both saw each other and then Chirag turned towards the bartender and shouted, "hey, man. Give me four shots please." He took the shots from the counter, had them and then returned the glasses and gave money to the bartender. All his friends then moved towards the dance floor. Both Chirag and Minnie were busy enjoying the party with their friends.

After sometime, Chirag and his friends were about to leave for home but suddenly Chirag stopped.

"Wait," said Chirag and turned back. He observed the place and got shocked. "I have seen this place somewhere." He contemplated and then realized, "yes, I saw this in my dream and that girl too. Where is that girl."

He started searching for her everywhere and couldn't find her. He then thought that maybe the dream was indicating something. Thinking about the same, he moved towards his friend's car and they left the place.

In the meanwhile, Minnie had reached the signal as she left the place a few minutes back. As she was waiting for the signal to turn green, it suddenly struck her that she had seen the place before and that boy too. She then decided to take a U-turn and thus quickly moved towards the disco so that she could find the guy. She reached the place and ran towards the bar counter searching for the guy. She saw all the corners but it was too late as the disk was half empty. Many people had left the place as it was very late. She then silently moved towards her car.

While on her way home, she muttered, "what a crap, man. I just missed it. If I met him, I would have grabbed his neck and told him not to disturb me in my dream again."

Chapter 7

The Nuclear lab

On her way back home, she felt happy as the day went pretty well, she then thought to use her powers and explore the places where no one could go if not invisible. She decided to go to a nuclear lab where all types of dangerous nuclear chemicals were kept to make explosives and were used in making war weapons.

She reached the spot and planned to take a long walk around the place. She parked her car at a place from where she could escape if things got worse and use it as an exit plan. Minnie started focusing on her emotions and then turned invisible. She moved towards the guard and stood in front of him. The guard smelled her perfume and uttered, "what a smell." Minnie grabbed that opportunity and stole the keys of the main gate.

As she moved forward, she thought whether she needed to enter from the main gate or should enter from the camera room. She finally decided and entered the camera room through a window. She silently stood and saw two more guards looking at the TV screen guarding the Lab. She slowly moved towards the door and realized that it was open, thus kept the keys on the floor as she didn't feel the need of it. She entered the main hall and was roaming here and there, seeing all the chemicals and was very much excited. Suddenly, a Doom sound was heard from the entrance. Minnie felt a vibration in the building and ran towards the window. She saw a group of gangsters killing all the guards. A few of them moved towards the camera room and were turning off the cameras so that no one could have any proof.

Minnie then saw the men entering the building. A few men held the head of the 'chief of the nuclear lab' and all gathered together as if awaiting someone's arrival. Minnie couldn't guess as to why they all stopped.

She then noticed two men in full suit entering the building; one was in black and the other in brown. It was somewhat like a ninja suit. Then all men moved towards the hidden chamber where a powerful nuclear chemical was kept which was used to change human habitability. The chemical could turn the human skin into stone in a way that no bullet or any kind of sharp object could enter and damage it. It could make hands and hair turn into spikes so that no one could hurt anyone easily. And it is also said that if this Liquid is injected with Sun Positive Energy then it can make all spikes into fire; turn hair and nails into fire. It's a Very dangerous innovation, if a good person has it, then it's secured, but if a bad person takes it then it can be the end of the Universe.

The men screened the chief's face and the door opened. The men started to take positions to guard the two Ninja's to complete the work. The two men went inside the vault, opened the bag and removed a device to unlock the vault. It was very tough because even a single mistake could cause life. The vault had a feature that if the lock did not open in the first attempt then the main gate would close. If the second attempt failed then the oxygen flow would stop and hazardous chemicals would start flowing from the wall and start melting objects in the room. If the third attempt got wrong, then all the walls would start getting closer and kill everyone present. If these situations arose, the nuclear bottle would automatically escape and change its position to another vault located in another place which was known only to the man who hid the vault.

Minnie was seeing everything silently and followed all the men. She then went inside the Vault when one of the ninja men was trying to extract the code. Minnie slowly raised her hand towards the touch screen to end the extraction, but the ninja guy immediately smelled her perfume. He stopped and turned towards his partner and asked whether he applied ladies' perfume. Minnie took the opportunity; pressed a button and moved away. Immediately, the door closed because the first attempt was failed and all three, were locked inside. The ninja guy then saw a thumbprint on the screen as if someone had pressed the screen. He then understood about the presence of someone in the room and acted as if he knew nothing. He indicated the same to his partner in their sign language and asked him to be silent. He contacted the guard outside instructing him to open the door. The guard outside screened the face of the chief again and the door opened. Minnie saw that the vault was designed in a manner that could trap anyone inside. She was then leaving and her eyes went on the touch screen. She said to herself, "oh my god, my thumbprint is on the screen." Even she was smart and thus planned another way to tackle the boys and went out of the vault. Both ninja guys were searching for the spray by which they could know the presence of any invisible being. One of the ninjas found it and sprayed it everywhere in the vault. Minnie smartly escaped the room and was waiting for the boys to begin the work again. The ninja man started to extract the code again and asked another ninja to keep an eye if anyone comes near them. He instructed him to stab the person if he senses the perfume again.

Outside the vault, Minnie went in a corner and turned back into her normal form. She then went near a guard who stood in the corner and looked straight in his eyes, waited for a few seconds and blossomed him. She then whispered in his ears to throw the chief's head on the ninjas and then shoot all his mates.

Following her instructions, the guard threw the head on ninjas. The ninjas were too quick to sense the object coming towards them and so they moved to their right to escape the hit. The head correctly landed on the touch screen and the code was not extracted. The second attempt was failed and thus the door closed again with the chemical flowing from the walls. Both the ninjas were stuck inside. Meanwhile, all the men were killed and the guard who was blossomed was killed by Minnie as she asked him to shoot himself. Minnie happily said, "job over" and started to walk towards the camera room and activated the cameras to record the movement. Inside the chamber, both the ninjas did not lose hope and started to extract it again because they knew if they lose the nuclear, then they would anyway die. Suddenly, a drop of chemical fell on the shoulder of one ninja and he screamed in pain because the chemical was so dangerous that it could melt and make a hole. The ninja covered the wound with his other hand and asked his partner to continue the extraction. The ninja happened to crack the code this time and saw that the chemical stopped, and the chamber opened without any disturbance. The ninjas took the bottle and kept it inside a briefcase safely. They came out of the chamber and saw all the guards were dead. They then looked at the cameras and found out that the cameras were activated, and the alarm started ringing.

Minnie saw in a camera that the ninja guys succeeded to steal the nuclear chemical and were running towards the camera room. She locked the room from inside and went out from the window and sat inside the car of the ninjas. The siren was heard and she became sure of the police approaching.

The police reached near the place and saw two people running very fast. The ninjas ran into their car and started to drive. As they were heading towards the exit gate to escape, Minnie came out from the open window and stood on the roof. She bent down and looked in the eyes of the ninja driving and blossomed him. She asked the ninja to pull the steering towards the extreme right. Apparently, the ninja pulled the steering towards the extreme right and Minnie jumped from the car and the car banged on the wall. Since both the ninjas were highly trained, they both left the car safely but were not able to pick up the briefcase and anyway escaped. The black one went to a nearby place where everything was dark so that the police could not find him with naked eyes, and the brown one climbed on the top of a tree and never moved so that they could not see him. Minnie silently took the briefcase and ran towards her car and left the place.

When the police arrived at the spot, they saw a car near the wall.

"If anyone is inside the car, better step out. You are surrounded by Police. Get out, raise your hands and kneel down." Said the police.

The policeman saw no one was inside and thus they went to the lab and started searching for evidences if any. On the contrary, Minnie was extremely excited and turned visible. She kept the briefcase under a tire in the car trunk and covered it with some shopping bags. She then moved towards her driving seat happily dancing and left for home.

Wooo hoooo, screamed Minnie while driving.

On her way home, a car passed by in which the black ninja was hiding. Minnie saw a man sitting in it in a black costume and ignored him. The black ninja also saw Minnie and ignored her, thinking some drunken girl was driving late night. He even saw the shinning number plate of Minnie's car with the letter M crafted on it, however he still ignored it. He was just waiting for the police to clear the area so that he could go to his boss SHADOW. Minnie reached and entered the home; she was blushing so much that she didn't even notice that Dhiraj was waiting for her on the sofa.

"Hello madam, what is going on, huh? My princess is so happy that she didn't notice her dad waiting." Said Dhiraj, keeping his book aside.

Minnie turned back, "Oh, sorry dad. I did not see you." Replied Minnie. "Thank you for such a wonderful life." She went near him and hugged him tightly.

"What is the reason of this happiness, my love? So, you finally found a guy, huh?" questioned Dhiraj.

"No, dad. It's just I had a very good day and enjoyed every moment. But why are you still awake?" replied Minnie.

"How can I sleep when my princess is not home. I cannot sleep without seeing you. The day I die, I want to see your face and see if you are in safe hands, then only I will peacefully go to hell because I will not get a place in heaven." Said Dhiraj.

"Oh, don't say like that. When I am near you no one can take you away from me. Don't worry, dad. I will never leave you and I am going to stay with you forever and yes, sorry to keep you awake this late." Replied Minnie

"I need to tell you something," said Dhiraj hesitatingly.

"Yes, Dad." Asked Minnie.

Dhiraj couldn't decide whether to tell her the truth about her past. He was afraid that if he told her, she would leave him and go. So, he said, “Good night. Sweet dreams. I love you.”

“I sense something fishy. I know you are trying to hide something, and I think I know what it is.” Replied Minnie.

“What will I hide from you? Everything is known to you; my all businesses, deals and everything. So, why will I hide anything?” said Dhiraj in a low tone.

“Ok, Dad. You may tell me whenever you feel is appropriate. Anyway, now go and sleep. You have a meeting tomorrow early in the morning. Sweet dreams.” Replied Minnie.

Subsequently, both went to their rooms. Minnie got freshen up and then happily slept off. On the other side, both the ninjas reached to shadow's place and told him everything that happened.

Dhiraj went into his room and kept contemplating whether he should tell Minnie the truth about her past. At the very moment, Dhiraj's phone rang and it was SHADOW.

“The work is not completed. Turn on the TV tomorrow at 8 am. And I want all the answers.” Said Shadow in an authoritative tone.

“Ok, I will see to it.” Replied Dhiraj.

In the contrary case, Chirag felt very exhausted when he reached home. He entered the kitchen, drank water, and then moved towards his room. As he entered, he just fell on the bed and went in a deep sleep.

Chapter 8

The Connection

The next morning, Dhiraj turned on the TV at around 8am. As he switched to a news channel, he saw the breaking news – "City's biggest secured nuclear lab under attack. All the guards found dead. Some other dead bodies found, and they appear to be trained commandoes. The most precious nuclear chemical made by Dr. Dhanush is missing and the police found his head cut and thrown in the chamber. 'We have some evidence, but we still need to find the person behind all this and we have appointed a special team who will definitely find the culprit.' Said the Police Official."

The media then interviewed another police official who was present at the spot last night. "We saw two people running from the entrance of the lab carrying a briefcase and sat in the car. We suddenly saw the car turn and crash into the wall. However, to our great surprise, when we reached the place, we found that both men and the briefcase were missing. According to me, there were three people, but we saw only two. Apparently, the third person would have taken the briefcase." Commented the Official.

The media then showed the camera recording of the two men taking the nuclear bottle in hand, keeping it in their briefcase and running out of the chamber and moving towards the exit gate.

Dhiraj immediately called Shadow and said, "Don't worry, I will handle the situation."

At the same time, Shankar was also watching the news channel and was stunned at seeing the symbol on the Ninjas' jackets. He went running to Chirag's room to check whether he was present or not. He took a sigh of relief as he found him sleeping. He then called Swati and showed her the symbol; it was Zexox's Symbol. Swati was taken aback and they both looked at each other with fear in their eyes.

"Did Chirag find something big?" questioned Shankar. Both Shankar and Swati went to Chirag's lab and saw everything, but they could not connect it with the incident, so they left the lab and decided not to say anything about it to Chirag.

That day, Chirag got up late and walked towards the drawing room.

"Good morning, dad. How are you? Asked Chirag.

When Shankar saw Chirag, he turned off the TV and replied, "Good morning. I am fine. How are you."

“What happened? Why did you turn off the TV? I want to see the news.” Replied Chirag.

Shankar started stammering and replied, “wa...what? No, nothing ha..happened. I was going to my room, so I turned the TV off, you also go and get ready.”

“Why are you behaving this strangely? I know you are hiding something from me. Come on. Said Chirag. “MOM come here. Look, dad is again hiding things from me.”

Swati came running in the drawing room and replied, “Enough is Enough. Shankar, tell him everything. We will need his help.”

“Help? What are you guys up to?” asked Chirag.

“Ok, listen to me. Let’s go to the lab and discuss the situation.” replied Shankar.

“Right now? That’s fine.” Said Chirag.

Chirag and Swati shook their head in the affirmative and followed Shankar towards the lab. Shankar opened the door, turned the lights on and asked them to sit.

“First, listen silently and do not interrupt.” Shankar started to explain the situation and ended by saying, “I THINK WE FOUND CHIARA.”

Both Chirag and Swati ran towards Shankar and hugged him happily. “Are you sure?” questioned Swati wiping her tears.

"I think so, I am still not confirmed. When I saw the camera clip of the incident, I only saw two ninjas running from inside the chamber. The question is how can a camera clip start from the middle? Also, the police said there were three people, however only two were seen. Amidst this, the briefcase was also missing. As I connect all these dots, it seems that the third person wasn't visible and thus I feel it was Chiara." Said Shankar and then showed the symbol of Zexox.

"This symbol is the reason behind the separation of you two and it was also present on the jackets of the Ninjas." He sighed.

"Ok, so our old enemy is back. Don't worry, dad. I will not spare him alive and will split him in two." Said Chirag rubbing his hands together.

"It's not that easy, my child. Keep your anger inside, don't show it and spoil the grudge. Wait for the right time and at that time show Zexox where his place belongs. For now, let's be happy of having a clue about your sister being alive." Replied Shankar.

"Ok, dad. Finally, we got a hint that my sister is alive, now that's great news." Chirag smiled.

"Chirag, you follow the symbol and try to reach to the boss, but don't use any powers or get caught." Said Shankar.

"Ok, sure." Promised Chirag.

Turning towards Swati, Shankar said, "Swati, let's go and call Raman and start making gadgets so that we can protect Chirag from the backside."

'All three dispersed and went for their tasks.'

Chirag took the photo of the symbol and went to Satish seeking help as he had contacts in the police. He reached Satish's office and explained everything to him. He then took the contact details of a police officer who could help him.

Chirag called the officer and said, "Hello, sir. I am Chirag, Satish's nephew. I need some help related to a symbol; can you guide me?"

"Yes, sure. Send me the picture and I will give you the details if I find any."

Chirag sent him the symbol's photo. The police officer replied that he feels he had seen the symbol somewhere. He then called Chirag and said, "I am giving you the address of a bar. Go inside, sit on a table and when the waiter asks for order, tell him 'the plate is hot; I need to sit on another table.' He will understand the code and take you to a powerful person. When you meet that person, tell him I have sent you and he will give you all the details. Stay relaxed, it's our area only."

"Thank you very much, officer. I owe you one favor." Said Chirag happily and hung the call.

Chirag went running towards his bike and jumped on it in excitement, but he did not know that getting the information was not that easy. He then started his bike and left for the Bar. He reached the bar, parked his bike, and went towards the entrance. The guards stopped him and said, “no Id no entry.” Chirag showed his Id and went inside. The bar was very well decorated. He found an empty table and sat comfortably. The waiter approached him and asked, “what would you have in drink, sir?”

“The plate is hot; I need to sit on another table.” Said Chirag in a low voice.”

“Follow me and do not utter a word.” Asserted the waiter.

The waiter took him towards the kitchen and pointed upstairs and said to the guard standing outside the kitchen entrance, “going to hell.” The guard opened the gate and said, “come back soon.” Both stepped to the hidden stairs and then reached the office and knocked the door three times leaving a gap.

‘Knock, knock, knock’

***

Back at Dhiraj’s place, Minnie got up late and came out of the room. She saw no one in the house and asked her servant to give her the breakfast with some hot milk as she was very hungry.

“Madam, it’s lunchtime. Shall I serve you lunch, or you wish to have breakfast?” asked the servant.

Minnie was shocked seeing the time as it was noon and thus asked her servant to serve the lunch. Minnie didn't go to office and decided to take some rest. With heavy eyes, she then went in her balcony and saw that her car was missing. She rushed downstairs and asked her driver, "where is my car?"

"Dhiraj Sir took it," replied the driver

"But why?" Questioned Minnie.

"His car was not working, and he was not in a good mood, so no one questioned him. He was watching the TV and then suddenly left without even having breakfast. In a hurry, he went alone and did not take any driver along." Replied the driver.

Minnie called Dhiraj several times, but he was not receiving the call. Minnie, in full tension turned on the TV and saw the news channel. The news was still showing the same incident that happened the night before. She somewhere realized that this was the topic Dhiraj was hiding from her. She thus waited for Dhiraj to come back home because no one knew where he went.

Dhiraj first went to meet the commissioner and spoke about the event. He was trying to get the detail of the 3rd person who took the briefcase, but Commissioner did not say a single word to him regarding that.

"If in this case you are anyway found involved, then you will be called a terrorist and I am sorry, no one in this world could save you. You will end up living your life in jail." Asserted the commissioner.

“No, no. It's not me. Don’t worry, I have come to support you and if you need any help don’t forget you have a friend.” replied Dhiraj and then left the office.

Next, he went to meet Shadow. He entered Shadow's hidden arena which was fully guarded. He then left his phone, gun and watch with the security and went towards the lift. As the lift arrived, he pressed ‘HELL’ on the touch screen and the lift then opened in the terrace area. He saw Shadow standing with his bodyguard Bozzo and the ninjas; Black and Brown.

“Ok, so you managed to escape. But what about the briefcase, how can you both be so careless and still stand with your boss?” questioned Dhiraj.

“Stop it, Dhiraj. You don’t know them. I trust them more than anyone. They both are my sons, Python and Paxton. They are saying that they felt the presence of a 3rd person and were on the verge of getting killed.” Replied Shadow.

“WHAT? Your sons got defeated? And who are they talking about?” asked Dhiraj.

“They say that it was a lady who was invisible and tried trapping them.” Replied Shadow.

“A lady? Did you say an invisible lady, or I heard it wrong? Really, how is it possible?” questioned Dhiraj and then stared at both the boys present there.

“Stop behaving like a fool and find the girl and the nuclear bottle.” Replied Shadow.

"Ok and how am I supposed to find the invisible girl in this big city?" said Dhiraj. "It will take time but still I will try to find her."

He then looked at the ninjas and said, "At least give me some clue so that it would be possible for me to track her." Python and Paxton looked at each other and then looked at Dhiraj and said, "Sorry, we never saw her. How are supposed to give you any clue?"

Dhiraj was very annoyed and thus left the place. As he went towards the lift to go down, Python followed him and said, "I will drop you till your car."

Both entered the lift and Python said, "the girl wore a great perfume which could be a limited edition." He then mentioned everything briefly. They both reached the ground floor and kept discussing about the incident.

"Ok, I will try my best," said Dhiraj and shook hands with Python. He collected his stuffs from the security and as he was moving towards his car, Python called him again and said, "Sorry, I missed an important part." Dhiraj went near him and asked him to say the same as every minute detail was important at that point.

"When I sat in the car and looked in the front mirror to see how far the cops were, then I saw that the seat was bent as if someone was sitting on it. Then when I started the car and began to move, I got a feeling as if someone was getting out of the window and went on top of the car. And when I turned to see if the cops were coming, suddenly my mind went blank and I heard a whisper asking me to turn the steering towards the extreme right and I banged the car on the wall and the briefcase was struck below the seat." Said Python.

Dhiraj, after hearing started to shiver. He was sweating very much and thus took out his handkerchief and started to wipe his sweat. At the moment, just one name stuck in his mind and that was Minnie. He then asked Python, "did you say anything about this to your dad?"

"Yeah, I did tell him. But why are you sweating so much? Even the Ac is on." Asked Python.

"Ah, nothing. Actually, I also experienced the same situation at my warehouse; my codes were missing, but I thought I was mistaken. However, after hearing you, one thing is clear; the invisible girl is real." Lied Dhiraj. "Ok, now I will have to leave, I have a meeting to attend." said Dhiraj and left the place.

"Ok, Dhiraj. See you soon." Replied Python.

Dhiraj's behavior was changed and he walked very fast towards his car. He reversed the car so recklessly that he was almost going to hit a guy who was crossing the gate. Dhiraj then adjusted his rear-view mirror to check if anyone was following him and drove towards his home.

Chapter 9

The Untold Truth

At the bar:A bulb above the gate turned Red and then Green. The waiter said, "From here you need to go inside, my work is done." Chirag opened the door saw a chair facing the front wall and the person was on call. The man on the phone then turned around and gestured him to sit by showing a hand signal. Chirag sat on a chair facing the man and greeted him.

"Mr. Sharma has sent me. I need some information regarding a symbol." Said Chirag politely and showed him the symbol. "May you please tell me where I will find this?"

"I hope you know gathering information is difficult." The man replied and cleared his throat.

Chirag kept a bundle of ₹50,000 on the table. The man was quiet and then looked at Chirag. Chirag understood and kept another ₹50,000 bundle on the table. The man then gave him the address of Shadow's residence. Chirag got up and turned towards the door. He was about to open the door when the man from the back said, "Try to stay alive."

"He doesn't have an idea of what is coming." Chirag smiled with his eyebrows raised and left the bar. He went towards his bike and left for the address. As he reached there, he parked his bike near a shop and walked towards the main gate. The gate opened and he saw a car being reversed and coming towards him in a very fast pace. Chirag saw the ninja standing on the building entrance and waving the guy in the car. He then ran towards his bike and started following the car. He saw that the car reached Dhiraj's place. He then saw Dhiraj moving out of the car and running towards the entrance of his home. He was surprised as in the past he had come to this place following the men whom he found at the location of the truck. After witnessing all this, he decided to go home and inform his dad about the same.

Back at shadow's place, Python was stunned seeing Dhiraj's behavior. When he went out, he saw the same car he witnessed yesterday and looked at the number plate and saw the creative M shinning on it. Python then thought that it might be Dhiraj's daughter's car and she must have been returning home after a party. He then went to his Dad and told him everything that happened between him and Dhiraj. Shadow called all his bodyguards and said, "we are leaving this place and going back to London. However, I need you to keep an eye on Dhiraj and update me all details."

"Why do we need to leave the place, dad? We will take the nuclear along and kill the girl." Said Python.

"You know all the techniques, but where were you when intelligence was distributed by God. You have grown up but still I have to clean your mess, so keep quiet and let's move to our homeland because the police have the bodies of our men with the symbol on it. The police can come at our doorsteps any time and catch us. Before that we must escape. We will execute the further plan from home."

"Ok, Dad. Let's move." Replied Python.

Shadow and his sons left for London and decided to operate the mission from home. They also informed Dhiraj about it via a messenger.

Dhiraj reached home and ran towards Minnie. He saw her sitting on the sofa eagerly waiting for him. He went near Minnie and held her hand tightly. He said nothing and pulled her in the room and locked the room from the inside.

"I need answers in yes or no." said Dhiraj in extreme anger.

"Ok but..." Dhiraj stopped her in between and said, "shut up. I'm speaking, right? I only need answers in yes or no. Later you will be asked for an explanation."

"Were you present in the nuclear lab building yesterday when the incident happened? Yes or No."

"Yes," replied Minnie biting her nails.

"Did you kill the guards?" questioned Dhiraj raising his eyebrows.

"Yes," replied Minnie in utter shock as to how Dhiraj knew about all the details.

Dhiraj was taken aback. "Did you attempt to kill the ninjas?"

"Yes," replied Minnie.

Dhiraj asked the next question, "Did you blossom the ninja driver?"

"Yes" was the answer again.

Dhiraj then lowered his tone and asked the final question, "Are you the invisible girl?"

Minnie looked straight in Dhiraj's eyes, fear no more rented in her heart. "After knowing everything, do you still want me to answer the final question?"

Dhiraj was stunned for a second and fainted. He could only utter, "we are finished". Minnie held Dhiraj and made him rest on her bed. When Dhiraj opened his eyes, he saw Minnie sitting on his side waiting for him to get up. He got up and hugged Minnie. "We are finished, beta."

"Stop it and nothing is going to happen when you have me." Replied Minnie.

"Do you know whom you have messed with? Said Dhiraj while rubbing his hands in tension.

"Who cares? You first have something and then we can continue the discussion. I need many answers from you." Minnie smiled.

Dhiraj was very hungry and thus agreed. “Now let’s leave whatever happened. Let's think about the solution.” Dhiraj completed his food and became normal.

“My first question, how do you know about yesterday’s incident and are you linked with it in anyway?” Minnie questioned politely.

Dhiraj then told Minnie everything; from meeting Shadow and the deal which they signed to the recent meeting he had with him. He then ended by saying that he wanted to tell something to her.

Minnie stood up in anger and said, “I have not finished yet. I have seen you since I was a child, I never saw you being so much greedy. What powers do you still require? You are already a powerful person in your city, is that not enough? Why do you need to rule the world paring up with a monster? Do you even realize the fact that once all this work gets over, Shadow will kill you and rule the world alone. On your words about him, he seems to be such a powerful person, then why will he need you after the work gets completed? You are just being used. You are a smart person, how can you fall in such a small trap and almost get yourself killed. Leave it to me now, I will manage the situation.”

Dhiraj lowered his gaze as he felt ashamed of what he did. “For a few more bundle of notes, I did not think of you and have put your life in danger. I’m sorry, my dear. Please forgive me and I am not and cannot be a good father to you. After all this, please don’t leave me alone.”

Minnie felt the pain in his voice and said with tears flowing down her eyes, "it's ok, dad. At least you've realized the mistake. I am not going anywhere, I will stay with you and you are the world's best daddy who gave me so much happiness. I love you, dad. Please don't change your mind again. And where did I get these powers from? I know you are hiding many things from me. I never asked you about my mom, but today I want to know everything, every detail. Please tell me."

"I don't know." replied Dhiraj emotionally. "Wait, I will be back." He got up from the bed and went towards his room and started searching for the bracelet. He found it and went back to Minnie's room. He stood on the door and saw Minnie facing the window.

"I never got married," said Dhiraj facing the floor and showed the bracelet to Minnie.

Minnie turned back towards Dhiraj in ultimate shock and replied, "WHAT? Then where did you find me? Am I an Alien?"

"You are not an Alien." Replied Dhiraj and narrated the entire life story from the very beginning.

Minnie had tears in her eyes. She hugged Dhiraj and started crying loudly. "You are the angel of my life. Thank you for raising me. You left everything just for me. I am speechless, dad."

"Come on, beta. It's ok. Now you are free to go wherever you want. I will manage Shadow. You go and live happily." Replied Dhiraj caressing her hair.

Minnie pulled herself back wiping off the tears. “I am not going anywhere. This is my house and you are my Dad, and the matter about Shadow, I will not spare him. You stay out of it and just give me a hand to make a full proof plan to destroy him. And yes, from now, it’s my responsibility to protect you. I will not let anyone even touch you.”

Dhiraj inhaled and smiled at Minnie. It was certainly a proud moment for him. “Ok, now you are the boss of this house. Everything will go as you like. Stay blessed, and may you find your parents soon.”

As he was about to leave the room, Minnie asked him to stop. “Here’s your gift, I hope it goes in the right hands.” She gave him the briefcase which she brought from her car while Dhiraj went searching for the bracelet. Dhiraj took the briefcase and said, “don’t worry, dear. I am on your side.”

Chapter 10

The Briefcase

Dhiraj took the briefcase and left the house. He moved towards the car and started for the Police Commissioner's home. When Dhiraj was on his way, he called the commissioner and said, "on the way to your home. It's urgent." Dhiraj reached the commissioner's place and knocked the door twice. He got no response and thought as to why was no one showing up. He again called the commissioner and could hear the phone ringing as he was just outside the gate. Dhiraj felt something strange and decided to call Minnie.

As he was about to dial Minnie, he saw a big shadow approaching towards him. He turned back and was surprised to see it was Bozzo; Shadow's bodyguard. Bozzo punched Dhiraj on his face and carried him on his shoulders as he became unconscious. He then called Shadow and informed him that the task was completed. As he was walking towards his car carrying Dhiraj and the briefcase, Chirag was standing on the entrance and said, "SUPRISE."

"Hey, you, small ant. Move from my way or I will smash you." Said Bozzo in a heavy voice, gesturing Chirag to move away.

"If I'm an ant, you might be an elephant. I will enter in your ear and kill you." Chirag laughed.

Bozzo got angry and threw Dhiraj on Chirag and tried to punch him. Chirag dogged both Dhiraj and the punch and said, "now it's my turn." Chirag got angry and turned into fire. Bozzo was shocked and stood there with a big question mark on his as if he saw a dinosaur in front of him and did not know what to do. Chirag then threw fireballs on Bozzo and injured him badly. However, he kept him alive so that the police could get answers. Chirag then became normal and carried Dhiraj to his car and subsequently carried Bozzo to the backseat. Chirag drove Dhiraj's car to the Police Officer friend and handed him Bozzo. "I owed you one favor and so I brought him to you, you can get more answers from him." He gave him the briefcase and said, "Your promotion is fixed. Here is the nuclear bottle which was stolen yesterday."

The police officer was shocked and wasn't able to say anything, but still managed to congratulate him. "Chirag, we need more brave people like you. Thank you very much. You saved the earth and have also saved many lives which were on stake."

"It's my duty and as a responsible citizen I have done my job and I expect the same from you. And I am sorry to say your commissioner is no more. Bozzo killed him and his family." Replied Chirag.

"A big loss for us." Replied the Officer. He then asked the police personnel to reach the Commissioner's place and also inform the ambulance so that the bodies could be sent for postmortem. Chirag left the place and took Dhiraj home along with him. When he reached home, Shankar opened the door and saw Chirag carrying someone. He thus asked, "who is he?"

"He is Dhiraj" replied Chirag walking slowly towards the lab. "When he gets up, we will get more answers." He made Dhiraj sit on a chair and tied him with a rope. Chirag then went into the kitchen, drank some water, and went to Shankar to explain everything. Shankar and Chirag went into the lab and stood facing Dhiraj. Chirag sprinkled some water on Dhiraj's face. Dhiraj slowly regained his consciousness and saw Chirag and Shankar standing in front of him covering their faces. Dhiraj then said, " you are that rat who entered my property and took photos. What do you want from me?"

"What a memory! Chirag started clapping. "So you still remember my face, huh. Start speaking the truth before I smash you."

"Go ahead. Smash me." Replied Dhiraj.

"You should be thankful that I did not hand you over to the police. You are sitting in front of me maybe because of your good deeds. So better speak the truth or we will not leave you."

Dhiraj tried to calm himself and then explained everything to Chirag. He then enquired about the briefcase to which Chirag replied that he had given that to the police. He also informed Dhiraj that the commissioner was no more.

"May his soul rest in peace," said Dhiraj in a low tone. "Thank you so much for saving me. By the way, how did you manage to bring the elephant down."

"That's a secret." Chirag smiled. "Well, we have decided to set you free."

Shankar held Dhiraj from the back and asked Chirag to close his eyes with a black cloth and cover his face with the same. Chirag then untied Dhiraj and said, "we will drop you home in your car." Shankar made Dhiraj unconscious by hitting him on his neck; he was an expert in that. Chirag and Shankar carried Dhiraj and put him in the car, and Chirag drove the car to Dhiraj's place. Shankar followed him by his car in order to bring Chirag back with him. They reached near the entrance and Chirag shifted Dhiraj on the steering and left the car. He made Dhiraj head down on the horn so that his people could come and take him inside.

Dhiraj's men came running outside hearing the horn sound and saw that it was Minnie's car and someone was on the steering. They removed the black cloth and saw it was Dhiraj. With tension running down their veins, they took him out and carried him towards the entrance.

“Minnie madam, please come out. See what has happened to Dhiraj sir,” shouted one of the men. Minnie came running and enquired about how it happened and who did it. “We don’t know, Madam,” replied the guard. Minnie asked the men to take Dhiraj to his room. The guards followed the instruction and carried Dhiraj to his room. Minnie waited the whole night for Dhiraj to get up. She was very concerned and was even worried about the briefcase.

Dhiraj woke up around 7 am and found Minnie sitting next to him. “What happened, are you fine?” asked Minnie while filling a glass of water for Dhiraj. He narrated the entire incident to Minnie and asked her to relax. “Now everything is at its place. Let’s take some rest and get back to work. We need to plan something about Shadow.” Said Dhiraj reassuringly.

“Thank god, you are safe.” Replied Minnie and then asked her servant to get the breakfast ready.

For a few days, everything went normal; the nuclear bottle was kept secured at another place and Dhiraj and Minnie too were safe and happy. They spent time with each other and were searching for new mom for Minnie. Shadow got to know that it’s not the right time to get involved so he waited for the right time to come into action. Bozzo was under the custody of the police but never opened his mouth. Shankar and Chirag on the other hand were restless as everything was too silent and it was irritating them.

Chapter 11
The Reunion

19th April

Everything was going smooth till date. Minnie and Chirag both after work went out with their friends. Minnie went to a nearby cafe whereas Chirag went to a park. As they went back home, they decided to sleep for some time and then, both went into the dreamworld.

Chirag: He saw Bozzo standing in front of him, fully suited and was fighting to bring him down.

Minnie: She on the other hand saw both the ninjas; the black one held a sword in his hand and the brown one held Dhiraj. Minnie immediately went invisible and was planning to save Dhiraj. She then saw that a man (Chirag) was fighting with someone (Bozzo), so she thought of helping the man so that in return he would help her kill the Ninjas.

Both got up from the sleep at the same time, it was 5 am sharp. They drank water and hoped that the dream doesn't come true.

In the meantime, Shadow sent the ninjas to set Bozzo free and made a device by which he could win the battle against Chirag. The Ninjas, with an invisible aircraft designed by Shadow directly attacked the prison. They killed the guards by firing shuriken so that other police guards could not react and then slowly killed all the police guards on top bunkers. Both the Ninjas asked the pilot to wait till they returned and then got down with the help of a rope. They reached down on the field where all the prisoners were resting in break time. The Ninjas looked around but couldn't find Bozzo as he was kept in the cell because he used to injure people whenever sent on grounds. Both the Ninjas, with their speed techniques and fighting skills killed everyone who came on their way and started searching for Bozzo. The ninjas found the cell, broke it and released Bozzo. All three ran towards the field and climbed the aircraft. They moved to a safe house where no one could find them and where they could train Bozzo with the new device. Everything happened so quickly that the police could not take any action.

After a few hours, Chirag got a call from the officer.

"Bozzo escaped the prison with the help of someone," informed the Officer.

"What? And where am I supposed to find him?" questioned Chirag angrily.

"I don't know, but you need to start the search. Let me know if you find something. I will call you later." The Officer disconnected the call.

Chirag felt clueless as to how he should begin the search. He thought of visiting Dhiraj's place to check if everything was fine. As he found everything ok, he went back home and waited to get any information.

Dhiraj saw everything on the TV the next day and informed Minnie about the same. Minnie assured him that Shadow's end was near and that she would handle the situation.

After a month, 19th May

Both the ninjas decided to kidnap Dhiraj, so they went to his home silently and climbed the wall easily with their skills. The weather wasn't good that day; a lot of thunder was heard. As the Ninjas reached the balcony, a thunder stroked the area and thus their shadow was visible on the opposite wall. Ignoring everything, they both entered Dhiraj's room and found him sleeping. They then put chloroform in a handkerchief and covered Dhiraj's mouth and nose. One of the Ninjas left a note on his side table. They put him in a bag and carried to their van, killing everyone who came in between. The next morning, Minnie's day servant entered the gate and screamed seeing blood spilled everywhere. She called the police. Minnie woke up hearing the scream, came in the balcony and saw blood everywhere. She ran towards Dhiraj's room and saw everything messed up. Dhiraj was missing and she then found a note of the table which read,

If you have guts, come alone in the address given below.

Minnie was already geared up and left for the place before the police could reach her place.

After sometime, the Police reached Dhiraj's place and saw everything. The Officer in-charge called Chirag and informed him about the incident. Chirag reached the spot and went in Dhiraj's room where he saw the note and thus decided to go to the safe house. Chirag called his dad and informed about the incident. He suited himself and left for the place.

Chirag knew all the possible shortcuts so he reached early and saw the guards outside ready to attack. Chirag became angry and lighted himself up and moved towards the guards. He started killing them one by one. All the guards were firing at Chirag but nothing happened as the bullet used to melt before it reached him.

At the same time, Minnie was seeing everything and was shocked. She was clueless as how can someone have such powers and she also turned invisible and entered the building. It was easy for Minnie to kill anyone coming in her way, she then moved forward and started killing all the guards, floor by floor and saw that the building was wiped out and she could not find the Ninja Brothers. Therefore, she ran down towards the main entrance. Chirag killed all the guards with his firepower.

Bozzo surprisingly came running from the entrance towards Chirag and sprayed water on him so that he could not light himself again. Chirag smelled the water and realized that some chemical was mixed in it. He saw Bozzo standing in from of him with a different gadget, a two-spray model. The buttons for its operation were on Bozzo's palms which were attached to a stainless-steel pipe on a cylinder. One spray had this chemical water to defuse the fire and the other had white paint to make any invisible thing turn visible. Bozzo's face and body were covered with a special suit designed by Shadow which would not allow the fire to pass. Chirag ran towards Bozzo and jumped on him trying to punch his face. However, Bozzo was so strong that he caught Chirag's hand in seconds and threw him away.

Minnie went to the security room and checked all the cameras to see where the Ninjas were hiding. As she scrolled the camera screen, she saw the Ninjas standing and Dhiraj hanging in front of them. Minnie thought of where the place could be. At the same time, a guard entered the security room and observed that the computer mouse was moving. He then moved his stick in the air to hit Minnie. Minnie understood that she was under attack so she suddenly moved right and caught the guard and asked him the way to go to the Ninjas. The guard told her the direction and the secret lift which would take one to that place. Minnie then killed the guard and saw the hidden lift. She contemplated not to go alone as it would be difficult to handle. Thus, she decided to help Chirag in defeating Bozzo and in return ask Chirag to help her to save Dhiraj. Minnie ran towards Chirag and stopped seeing Bozzo. She slowly moved towards Bozzo and removed the pipe from the tank. Chirag was dried by then and again lighted himself up and threw a fireball. Bozzo saw the fireball coming towards him and pressed the button for the liquid to pass, but the liquid did not come. He kept pressing the button but soon realized that the pipe was disconnected and all the liquid was spilled on the ground. The fireball didn't stop and hit his face. Chirag kept firing more and more.

Minnie from the other side tried to blossom him but was not able to because the suit did not let any energy pass through it. She then decided to tear the suit apart and it was only possible if she could break both the cylinders so that the stitching could loosen and the suit could be removed. Bozzo knew that only Minnie could have disconnected the pipe. As Minnie was about to hit the cylinder with the sword, Bozzo acted as he was busy fighting with Chirag, but suddenly turned around and sprayed the white paint on Minnie. Due to the paint, she was a little visible and Bozzo kicked her and the sword was in the air. Chirag caught the sword and attacked on the cylinder, both the cylinders broke and the suit became loose. Minnie then jumped towards Bozzo and pulled the suit out while Chirag held Bozzo's hand so that the suit could come out easily.

Chirag was totally shocked sensing someone invisible around and couldn't control his happiness as he understood it was his sister. He again started firing the balls. Bozzo was not able to escape and was killed. Minnie became normal and both Chirag and Minnie celebrated the moment by clapping. They suddenly stopped facing each other and both asked each other at the same time. "Why do you come in my dreams?"

"Forget it now and let's go. I need to save my dad, he is in the hands of the Ninja brothers." Said Minnie.

"Dad? But our dad is at home?" replied Chirag.

"Our dad? What do u mean?" questioned Minnie.

"Silly girl. You are my sister." Said Chirag smilingly.

"What are you blabbering?" asked Minnie in shock.

"Ok wait." Chirag then took his bag and searched for the bracelet. He then showed her the bracelet and told everything.

Minnie hugged Chirag and said, "why it took you so long to find me?"

"Now leave all this and let's go to our dad first. We shall discuss everything at home." Replied Chirag.

"What? No, let's go and save my dad." Asserted Minnie.

Chirag was very excited to take her home and thus asked, "Why do you need to save an evil man?"

Minnie slapped him and said, "he is the only one because of whom you can see me standing alive today, so stop all this and come along or you go home and I will go save him."

"Ok, I'm sorry. I got way too excited, let's go and save Dhiraj." Chirag smiled.

Chirag and Minnie ran towards the secret lift and pressed the button and went up. The lift opened and they saw both Ninjas waiting for them. "Welcome-Welcome. How did you like the trap, huh. Enjoyed?"

"Where is Dhiraj?" asked Minnie and the Ninjas showed them that he was hanging on the ceiling with blood dripping from his wrist. One of the Ninjas said, "after seeing the lift moving up, I understood that you are coming so I just did the inauguration and cut his nerve. You both have 1 minute to save his life and I bet before you reach him, he would be dead."

Chirag lighted himself and started throwing fireballs on the Ninjas but it was not effective as they were very fast and the aim missed every time. Minnie turned herself invisible so that no one could see her and started moving towards Dhiraj. Paxton was standing facing Dhiraj, therefore she silently tried to pass by. Paxton felt her presence and he suddenly kicked her exactly on her stomach and she feel away. Both Chirag and Minnie were finding it difficult to defeat the Ninjas as they were very fast and their fighting skills were stronger than Mi-Chi. The ninjas had glasses given by Shadow which helped them identify Minnie. The glasses used to beep when anyone was standing near them. They also used their shuriken on both Mi-chi and even used their swords to attack. Mi-Chi both were able to dodge the attack and then Chirag went towards his bag and became normal. He decided to use his dad's gadget and thus took it out and wore it in both hands. He then called Minnie and said, "throw any object towards the Ninjas and I will make it huge so that they cannot dodge it." So Minnie hit a wall with a chair and started throwing the broken pieces on the Ninjas. Chirag used to make them large and the Ninjas did not know what to do. They were injured and thus fell on the floor. Minnie then started to throw any object that was near her and Chirag used to make it huge. Many a times the

Ninjas dodged the objects too. Seeing all this, Minnie and Chirag made a plan to make both the Ninjas stand near the wall so that Chirag could make the object big and crush them on the wall. Mi-Chi succeeded in bringing the Ninjas near the wall and Minnie then threw a piece of brick towards the Ninjas and Chirag made the brick turn into a huge piece. The brick hit the Ninjas and Minnie jumped and gave more pressure on the brick. The wall crushed the Ninjas and finally they were defeated by Mi-Chi.

Minnie ran towards Dhiraj, un-tied him and rested his head on her lap and asked Chirag to cover the wound with some cloth. Chirag ran towards his bag and took out his handkerchief, tore into two and covered the wound. Minnie kept crying asking Dhiraj to open his eyes but when she touched his nerves the pulse was too low. "I am sorry. I left you alone even after knowing about the prison attack. Dad, please open your eyes."

"Let's take him to the hospital before it's too late." Said Chirag consoling Minnie. Chirag carried Dhiraj on his shoulders and moved towards the lift. As they reached the ground floor, both ran towards Minnie's car. Minnie sat along with Dhiraj in the backseat and Chirag drove to the hospital. When they reached the hospital, Chirag came out of the car and called the staff. The staff came running with a stretcher and they carried Dhiraj to the operation theater. The Nurse called the doctor who was attending a patient and informed him about the emergency. The doctor ran towards the operation theater.

The doctors anyhow managed to save Dhiraj, but he was still critical because too much blood was lost and even if they injected new blood, it would take time to activate the organs and keep him alive. After sometime, Dhiraj opened his eyes and asked the doctor to allow him to meet Minnie once. The Doctor agreed and went out to convey the same to Minnie. She went inside holding Chirag's hand.

"He is my brother, Chirag." She left Chirag and went near Dhiraj. "I want you to please fight back and come back to life. You are the most important to me, Dad."

Dhiraj smiled after hearing Minnie and said, "remember, once I told you that I cannot sleep without seeing your face. And thankfully, today God showered his blessings on me that I could regain consciousness and see you so that I could sleep well finally."

"Nothing will happen to you, Dad. The Doctors are trying their best and save you." Minnie held Dhiraj's hand and rested her head on the bed.

Dhiraj then blessed Minnie by raising his hand as a gesture of blessing her. He then closed his eyes and the hand fell on bed. Minnie screamed, "Dad." She was not able to accept the fact that Dhiraj left her. Chirag held Minnie and gave her the required support. Then both Mi-Chi went outside and Chirag made Minnie sit on a chair nearby. "Wait here, let me complete all the formalities so that we can take Dhiraj home." Said Chirag and went to the doctors.

After all the formalities, they took the body home and completed all the rituals. Chirag till then hid about Minnie from Shankar as he felt it was not the right time.

After a few days, Chirag went to meet Minnie and said, "let's go to our home, mom and dad are waiting."

Minnie was not able to come out from the incident and replied, "this is my home and I will not go anywhere."

Chirag sat beside Minnie and gave a paper with an address written on it and said, "I knew you would say this so I am giving you the paper with our address on it. It's ok if you want to take time, I can understand your feelings. Come home whenever you feel like." Chirag got up and was moving towards the gate when Minnie called him, "ok, wait. I will come home with you, but I will operate Dad's office from here only."

"You just come. All that you say is accepted." Chirag smiled.

Both then went home together. Swati opened the door and saw Chirag standing with a girl with luggage in hand.

"You got married and did not think to inform your parents. This was the thing we raised you for?" said Swati and went inside.

"Stop it, mom. Please go and call dad." Minnie smiled by covering her face.

"Shankar, come out of the room and stop meditating. Nothing is going to happen. See your son, he has brought his wife home and did not inform us even." Shouted Swati.

Shankar in shock got up and ran towards the door seeing Chirag. "Get out of my house."

Minnie started laughing loudly and said, “crazy family.”

“Hold on guys. She is Chiara, your daughter.” Replied Chirag.

Both Shankar and Swati were shocked. All they could utter was, “are you serious?” They got emotional and hugged Chiara. “Welcome home.” Greeted Swati.

“Not fair, guys. You got your daughter and so you forgot me.” Chirag kept the bag on the floor and stood folding hands.

All three; Shankar, Swati and Chiara started laughing. “Come here,” Said Shankar. All four members hugged each other.

“Dad and Mom, have a seat. I need to tell you people something.” Replied Chirag and then told them everything clearly.

“Don’t worry. First we shall plan against Shadow and bring him down.” Said Shankar.

Minnie too closed all the businesses but construction and looked after it.

All four lived happily together.

End of Part 1

Part 2

Chapter 12

Connecting the dots to Evil

13th July 2017. It was a sunny day and so Minnie and Chirag decided to go out on a picnic. They decided to call their friends at home, then book a van and go together. It was a sudden plan and as it's said, sudden plans are always a success. All the friends gathered and went to a nearby hill station and booked a resort which had all indoor and outdoor facilities. They all spent the day enjoying with each other. The next day, in the afternoon, after lunch, they decided to go home and take rest so that they could attend the office the next day. They reached home around 8 pm and all others dispersed to their homes.

As said, 'When everything in life is perfect then it's a sign of a storm coming towards you.'

Amidst all this, a guy in black suit followed them everywhere and he was so sharp in his work that the Twins never noticed his presence as they were so much involved in the trip. All the information was passed to his boss. The boss instructed him to call a few men and assign them the task to keep a watch on Chirag and Minnie's best friends. The guy in the black suit called his men and shared the targets' photos and address. First target was Chirag's friend and another was Minnie's friend. The men followed the friends.

Mi-Chi reached home, sat with their parents and shared the trip experience. They then went to their respective rooms. As Minnie went to her bed to sleep, Dhiraj's face flashed in and she got up with tears in her eyes. She got emotional and thought of going through her old photo albums. She got up from her bed, went towards the cupboard and took out the photo albums. As she sat on the bed seeing the pictures, she heard a knock.

"Shall I come in?" Chirag kept knocking the door.

"Yes, come." Minnie tilted her head looking at the door.

"I missed you." Chirag stepped in and closed the door.

"Oh…but I never missed you." Said Minnie teasing him. She kept the albums aside.

"What? Really." Chirag gaped.

"Obviously, when I never met you then how can I miss you? But I often saw a boy in my dreams and I used to think about him but never knew who he was. Said Minnie. "I even felt a connection with him."

"What a coincidence! I also saw a girl in my dreams." Exclaimed Chirag and started looking at the albums kept aside. "How the hell is this possible? This is the girl whom I often saw in my dreams, is that you?"

"Seriously? Yes, these are my pictures." Minnie looked at Chirag shockingly.

Chirag got up and ran towards his room and searched for his photos. He came back running to Minnie carrying his photo album.

"Is this the boy you used to see in your dreams?" Asked Chirag pointing at his teenage picture.

"Oh, yes. This is the boy." Asserted Minnie.

Both looked at each other and started laughing.

"That means we both were internally connected and knew each other. What a tragedy!" said Chirag and laughed.

Chirag and Minnie then discussed about their first meeting in the mall and then the Disco night and finally talked about the Ninjas. They laughed together and enjoyed the moment together. Both then decided that they'd share their dreams with each other so that they could solve problems beforehand, if any.

"Now I need to go to bed, I am exhausted. Good night." Said Chirag smilingly.

"Good night, brother." Replied Minnie.

As Chirag left, Minnie saw Dhiraj's photo and murmured, "good night, dad." She kept the album on the desk and went to sleep.

Minnie slept and travelled to the dream world. She saw Dhiraj and ran towards him. Dhiraj held Minnie's hand and said, 'come, I need to show you something.' He took her to their villa and they walked towards his room. He took her near his cupboard and opened it, pushed all his clothes to the left and a screen popped out in front displaying, 'enter the password.' Dhiraj then typed 'Minnie' and pressed enter. The door opened and both moved inside. Dhiraj said, 'Minnie, you need to dig my past to know what is inside.' Minnie then saw Dhiraj slowly moving away and waving at her saying, 'I will come back soon.'

Minnie suddenly woke up from the nightmare and noted all the details in her notebook so that she could not forget anything. She started to walk around the room thinking why did Dhiraj come in her dream and what did he want her to know. She decided to know everything about Dhiraj's past so she took her phone and called one of her servants.

"Do you have Gopal's contact number?" Minnie kept walking around.

"Who Gopal?" the man replied.

"Gopal; the guy who was the first servant and was very close to Dhiraj." Replied Minnie biting her nails.

"Sorry, madam. I don't know any Gopal. I joined the work late and never heard about any such person." The servant replied.

“Okay, then can you find the guy, I want to ask him something?” Questioned Minnie.

“I will try my best and if I get anything, I will surely get back to you.” Replied the servant.

Minnie then hung the call and thought of asking Chirag for help. She then went to Chirag's lab and saw he was busy making some gadgets with Shankar. She knocked the door. Chirag turned back and saw Minnie standing with a question on her face.

“What's the matter?” asked Chirag in a clueless tone.

"I hope I am not disturbing you, are you busy doing something? Can I talk to you for a moment?" Minnie kept rotating the knob of the door.

"Why not." Chirag smiled and told Shankar that he would join back in sometime.

Chirag and Minnie both went towards the living room and sat beside each other.

"Yes madam, how may I help you?" Chirag teased her.

Minnie told everything to Chirag. “We need to clear this before any huge problem occurs.”

“Let’s dig out then. Where do you need to start from?” asked Chirag.

"Hmmm... I want to know about Dhiraj; where he came from, how did he get so much Bounty and how did he live such a luxurious life." Minnie kept playing with her handkerchief.

"Oh, so this is annoying you? Don't worry, let's go then." Replied Chirag.

"Where are you taking me?" Minnie kept looking at Chirag.

"Where are you taking me?" mimicked Chirag and started laughing. "Your problems are my problems, come, I will take you to a person who will dig out everything."

"Ok, let's go." Replied Minnie with excitement.

As they both started moving out, they met Swati in the corridor.

"Mom, we will be home soon, we are going to dig something." Chirag smiled.

"Ok, come back soon." Replied Swati.

Both Chirag and Minnie then went to meet the Police officer.

As the police officer saw Chirag approaching near on the bike, he stopped him and waved smilingly. Chirag stopped the bike in front of the Officer.

"What's new, boy?" The officer looked at Minnie. "She seems familiar to me."

"Nothing special. I just came to trouble you." Chirag smiled. "She is my twin sister Minnie." Said Chirag pointing his finger towards Minnie. He then parked the bike outside the police station and walked towards the officer.

"Ok, where was she? I never saw her in your home? The officer kept thinking about something. “No, no, wait. I have seen her somewhere."

"I used to work with Dhiraj and you visited us for some case related to Max." replied Minnie.

"Yeah, now I remember. That day I came to you regarding some issue at the construction site created by Max. Sad to hear about Dhiraj. RIP," said the officer.

"I want dig out details about Dhiraj, so that I can find the link between Dhiraj and Shadow." Requested Minnie.

“Why not. Come, let's go in my office and talk about it." The officer started walking towards the station followed by Minnie and Chirag.

They entered and the officer asked them to have a seat. He then asked, "what information do you need?"

"I want to know every detail of Dhiraj; how did he become from a man of nothing to a man of everything." Replied Minnie in a heavy voice.

The officer called his assistant and asked him to bring all the files related to Dhiraj: the contractor. The assistant then logged in his computer and searched for ‘Dhiraj: the contractor’ in his crime folder and found that a big list appeared in front of him. The file displayed: ‘the location of the file is kept in main Commissioner's ward row number E vi Lower shelf.'

"Sir, all the files are in commissioner's wing and it will take a day for me to get permission and to fetch the files, shall I start the process?" Said the assistant standing near the entrance.

The officer nodded and then looked at both the twins. "Come tomorrow around 3 pm and take the files. Commute by your car as you will have to carry a lot of files because the complete E row lower shelf is filled with Dhiraj's file."

Minnie and Chirag looked at each other and nodded their heads in agreement to the terms and stood up saying, "Thank you officer." Both Mi-Chi then exited the building and sat on their bike.

"Did you listen to what he said? The 'E vi Lower shelf' sounded as EVIL."

Minnie knew that Chirag was mocking her and so she hit him on his shoulder and said, "Shut up and drive home." Chirag nodded with a smile and drove home.

The guy in the black suit was still following them and reported everything to his boss who then instructed to appoint a man to follow the officer as well. The guy shared the officer's details to his man instructing him to follow the officer and told him to wait for the call. The man agreed and followed the Officer.

Chapter 13

The Cube

As Chirag and Minnie reached home, they were shocked seeing the door half-open and some broken furniture thrown outside. They both ran towards the door and saw the house was all messed up with all the furniture broken. The TV was kept on with the news channel on screen.

Chirag ran towards the lab and saw blood on the floor; he then followed the blood spots and saw that it was heading towards the hidden door. He opened the door and searched everywhere but found nothing. It seemed to him as if Shankar wanted to say something but it was not clear.

Minnie on other hand was taken aback after seeing the news which stated: 'an invisible jet destroyed the nuclear lab and disappeared in the sky.' She then went in search of Swati but couldn't find her anywhere in the house. As she entered the kitchen, she screamed, "Chirag, come hear quickly. I found a note on the wall written with blood."

Chirag ran towards Minnie and was numbed on seeing the message on the wall with an arrow drawn pointing towards the clock.

"Round goes the clock, and time comes to all, when it comes, worse happens."

Chirag and Minnie looked at each other with sheer terror. Minnie then asked Chirag, "now what are we going to do?"

She again looked at the wall and asked Chirag to bring a stool in order to reach the clock to check if they find any note behind the clock. Chirag climbed on a stool and took the clock but found nothing. Minnie again looked at the time and said, "it is 2:00 am in the clock." She kept analyzing the wall and asked Chirag to put the clock again in its old position. Chirag agreed and put it in its old position.

"The number 2 could signify our mom and dad. But what is the arrow trying to indicate?" Said Minnie looking at the wall. She then noticed a hole in the wall and asked Chirag to reach the hole and search for some clue. Chirag reached the top of the wall near the hole with the support of Minnie by standing on her shoulders. He searched inside the hole and found a cube. He jumped on the floor and showed the cube to Minnie and asked, "now what? Do we need to solve this?"

"Give me the cube. You go and call uncle, let's see if he can help us." Minnie took the cube in her right hand while Chirag left to call their uncle.

Chirag called their uncle but he was not picking the call and so he decided to rush to his office.

In the meantime, Minnie was standing with the cube observing it carefully. The cube was a different one with some numbers on it. She started to search about it on the web, but she found nothing. She kept staring at the cube murmuring to herself, "six numbers that means crack six codes to find the destination." She then kept the cube on the table.

Satish rushed into the house with Chirag and was shocked at seeing the condition of the house. As he saw Minnie, he immediately asked, "did you find anything?"

Minnie nodded and showed him the cube. Satish saw the cube and asked, "did you find a way out?"

"I think we have to press a button so that we can get our first clue." Replied Minnie.

"Ok. Let's try, go ahead." Satish crossed his fingers.

Minnie pressed the button numbered 1. The cube started to change its direction and all the numbers went backside, and on the front side, a small box exactly opposite to number 1 opened with a paper coming out. She took the paper and suddenly the screen on the top side of the cube got activated with a display: 'task to be completed.' Minnie clicked on the screen, and a list of 6 items appeared as shown below, and an arrow pointing next page on the screen appeared and she then pressed next.

S.no	Item Name	Place	Place of origin
1.	The Magical mirror Size – 5feet weight 15kgs	The mirror of Queen Alice W/o King. Andrew (Famous Museum name The Historic House)	Greeworld
2.	Sunshine capture Height 2feet weight 150 kgs	Real owner is Queen Alice, Captured by A Paris king name Romeo after defeating King Andrew. (Lab of Science and technology)	Pary city
3.	Convertor of light to liquid 2.5 feet height long, weight 100kgs	Scientist Dr. Wilson lobo Richest man of Calton city Mr. Noha Ollivia	Carlton city
4.	CNC Machine to formulate and mix chemicals. Height 2 feet and weight 300kgs	Designed by a Scientist name Henry Wilson (Deep hidden in caves of forest)	The dark Forest (somewhere in east)

5.	Connecter	To be designed by Minnie	Inland
6.	Nuclear liquid	Made by Dr. Dhanush, Nuclear Lab Goa	Inland

Remember, every time you complete a task, you should take the cube along with you and press the center button on a symbol drawn, on the screen you need to enter the task done by entering codes as written below and press submit. Then, a location will be shown and you need to follow the location and place the object and go back home. After I receive the object, one of your loved ones will be delivered to you. Remember, if you type the codes beforehand and no object is found then your loved ones will never be seen.

Code for task #1 – ZS001
Code for task #2 – ZS002
Code for task #3 – ZS003
Code for task #4 – ZS004
Code for task #5 – ZS005
Code for task #6 – ZS006

Minnie got frustrated and said, “Really, we save the world and he wants us to rob it, now that’s insane.”

"Sometimes we need to make decisions which are not easy to swallow. And trust me, everything happens for good." reassured Satish with tears in his eyes.

"Good? We are going to be listed in the most wanted criminals and that's not a good sign for us." replied Chirag in frustration.

"I know that, but if we want our loved ones back, then we need to do something." Said Satish.

"Who the hell is this person? I am not going to spare him." Minnie sat on the couch helplessly.

Chapter 14
The Kidnapped

All three heard a tik-tik sound and looked around to search for the source. Suddenly Minnie saw the cube and said, "it's the cube." They looked at the screen of the cube where a timer was displayed with a date; 13th October 2017. As Minnie clicked on the arrow on the screen, a message displayed:

> You better hurry. Get all the things done before time because if the time exceeds, you may lose your loved ones one by one.

"Now that's not a good sign and what does he mean one by one? Wait, how many people has he kidnapped? Let's check that first." Said Minnie shivering in panic.

Chirag noticed the symbol on the cube and said, "this is Shadow's symbol. I know it very well."

"What? Are you sure?" asked Minnie in shock.

Satish looked at the symbol and said, “No, Chirag. It’s Zexox’s symbol.

“Hold on guys, first decide whose symbol is it and who is Zexox?” questioned Minnie.

“No uncle, it’s Shadow’s symbol because a few days ago I went to meet a guy for getting some information and he gave me Shadow’s address. I happened to see this symbol at his place.” Said Chirag reassuringly.

“Son, you have come in this world much later, I have seen this symbol for many years and cannot forget it. This symbol was the cause of you and Minnie getting separated.” Satish kept his right hand on Chirag’s shoulder.

“Ok, so both the enemies have teamed up and are trying to take revenge. Don’t worry, we will teach them a good lesson, but for now, let’s check how many of our known ones have been kidnapped.” Said Minnie.

Satish and Chirag then received calls at the same time; Satish got a call from Raman’s wife whereas Chirag got a call from his friend's mother.

Satish picked up the call and heard a loud cry, “Hello, Satish. Raman has been kidnapped and I don’t know who they were and where they have taken him. I called Shankar but he didn’t answer my call. I got your number so I called you. Please do something.”

“Shankar and Swati are also missing. Don’t worry, we will find everyone soon. I will call you if I find anything and please stay calm and don't go to the police." Requested Satish.

As Chirag received the call, he heard his friend's mother crying and breathing heavily. "My son has been kidnapped and the guy told to contact you and not the police, Where have they taken my son?"

"Aunty, even my mom and dad are missing and we are working on it. You please calm down and don't worry I will surely bring him back." Chirag disconnected the call.

Minnie also called her friend and got the same news of kidnapping from her friend's mother.

"Ok, so he is playing with our emotions. The total comes down to five people, but who's the sixth person?" Satish walks around contemplating. He then calls his wife Anu but she didn't answer the call. He tried calling on his landline but no answer was received. With tension running high, he rushed home which was nearby and found everything messed up. Anu was missing. He returned to Mi-Chi and said, "The sixth person is my wife, Anu." He sat on the stairs helplessly. "Let's go to my friend who is a brilliant officer, he will surely help us out."

All three ran towards the car keeping the cube at home and drove towards the police station. As they reached the place, they found the police station was messed up, all the constables were badly injured and were lying on the road. A few ambulances were around and the media was covering the scene.

“Oh my god! What has happened here?” said Satish in shock.

The assistant came running towards Chirag and said, “our officer has been kidnapped by some strangers who wore black uniform.”

“That’s a big problem. All our sources have been taken in custody. What are we going to do now?” Satish hit the steering.

All three left the place with disappointment and drove towards home. When they entered home, they were irritated by the tik-tik sound.

“How are we going to stop this sound? It's irritating, I cannot focus if it goes on.” Minnie pressed number 2 in an attempt to stop the sound. The sound stopped and a message popped, ‘first task incomplete, second task will be activated after the first task ends.’ Minnie threw the cube in anger. “Cut the crap and stop your nonsense.”

Chirag took the cube and hid it in the secret room which was in his lab. He kept it under the bed so that the sound could not be heard.

All three sat together and held each other’s hands to strengthen the support and motivate one another.

“Wait, wait. We still have a person who is the father of all these enemies, he can surely help us out, but I don’t know how should we contact him now.” Satish got up from his seat.

"Oh, that's a great news uncle. Who is he?" Minnie sniffed.

"He is the one because of whom you both have these powers and that great guy is none other than JOI." Exclaimed Satish.

"JOI? Who is he? And how are the powers related to him?" asked Chirag raising his eyebrows.

"JOI is an asset for us. Shankar once saved his life and he did not know that JOI was the king of Aries planet. One day JOI came to Shankar and said, 'you didn't know me and still saved my life. You surely have a golden heart and remember, in life if you ever face any problem, I am always with you.' He then gave Shankar a device and said, 'contact me only when you think you cannot do it yourself.' I was with Shankar at that moment so I know all this. Now the problem is how we are going to contact him?"

Mi-Chi both started staring Satish with a big question mark on their faces.

"Why are you kids staring at me? Come, let's find out how can we contact JOI." Satish started walking towards the lab.

Both nodded and followed Satish to the lab.

Chapter 15

Quest for Clues

“What was my parents’ role before I was born? Were they having some powers?” questioned Minnie.

“Do you think it’s the right time to explain this, because we have very limited time. So, for now, let’s focus in the present and search for the device to contact JOI.”

“Yeah, you’re right. Let’s search for it.” Nodded Minnie.

Satish was a computer expert and thus cracked the password of Shankar’s computer and started searching for a clue to contact JOI.

In the meantime, Chirag started following the blood drops and observed it directing towards the secret room, so he went inside and began searching for some clue. As he started to move away, his eyes went on a note written under the table. Chirag ran towards it and shouted, “uncle,

Minnie, come here." Satish and Minnie went running towards Chirag. "I need you to see this."

After observing the drawing, Satish instructed Mi-Chi to search the house in order to find the device. "Chirag, you go upstairs and begin searching and Minnie you go and make a plan for our first task." Mi-Chi nodded. "We three cannot do just one work, we need to split the work."

Minnie followed the same and started devising plan for their first task. On the other hand, Chirag went upstairs.

While searching for JOI's device in the lab, Satish asked Minnie, "what is shadow up to? Why does he need all these items? Can you ascertain the same?"

"I am a top student in nuclear science and according to me he is creating a set up to make himself the most powerful and so that he can rule the world without any fear." Minnie kept writing something in her notepad.

"And how is that possible?" asked Satish.

"Ok, I will explain it to you." Minnie carried the paper to Satish. "He will first set up a mirror in a slant position near the window and also set up a sunlight capturer attached to the liquid converter, and then connect it to the

CNC machine and finally set up a connector bed. The process will start after the lunar eclipse ends, that is on 13th October 2017. The first rays of the sunlight after eclipse will directly hit the mirror and will pass through the mirror reaching the device called sunlight capturer. The work of this device is to separate negative and positive energy and pass both light towards liquid converter. The liquid converter will convert both positive and negative light into liquid and will be stored separately. The negative energy forms the nuclear chemical that is to be purified before human trial because it cannot be directly injected as it will create a reaction and kill the person." Satish was taken aback. "Next is the CNC machine in which both the nuclear chemical and positive liquid will be combined with the help of a formula and become one unit. A single error in the formula can destroy the whole lab and turn it into ashes." Minnie gestured ash by rubbing her index finger and thumb. "Last but not the least is the connector by which the chemical will be diverted in five directions through a pipe connected to syringes for injecting. One by one, the injection begins; first one in right leg nerve, second in left leg never, third in right hand, fourth in left hand and last one near the neck nerve. The by pressing the flow switch, the liquid will start flowing and go inside his body from all five directions. It will reach his stomach and get mixed with the stomach acid and then the reaction will start. For a minute nothing will be felt but later he will never feel hungry, his skin will start becoming hard like stone, his hair on hand will turn into spikes with flames, his eyebrows will turn into spikes, his nails will also turn into sharp claws with flames and thus he would become the most powerful and unstoppable person in the world.

Satish stood there flabbergasted, completely clueless.

"Is this all even possible?" asked Satish.

"Yes, it is possible. And we can stop this from happening only if we replace the negative chemical with the correct nuclear chemical as it would lead to Shadow's death." Replied Minnie

"And how are we going to replace it?" questioned Satish.

"Don't worry, I have a separate plan for it." Minnie went towards the desk and sat down.

Satish called Chirag and said, "go to your dad's room and search for the device, if you find it, bring it to me and don't operate it."

Chirag agreed and went to Shankar's room in search for the device.

Back in the lab, Satish said, "I think Shankar was trying to indicate something through the symbol of home. According to me, home means a place where we started the journey, so I need to go to the old place where Shankar and I used to work and also look in other places if I can find anything. It will take me two days so till then you make a full proof plan for our first task and I will try to find that device."

"Ok, let's give it a try. You should take Chirag along with you, if God forbid anything worse happens, he will safeguard you." Replied Minnie.

"No, there is nothing to worry the place. It is a silent place and I don't think anything can happen, let Chirag search around if he finds something." Said Satish.

"Ok, no problem. You carry on and I will be here in the lab if you need any help." Minnie got up from her place bidding Satish a goodbye.

As Satish turned around to move out, his leg hit the furniture and he immediately sat down in pain. Minnie heard the sound and went running towards him. "What was that sound?" asked Minnie and sat next to Satish.

"I was in a hurry and did not see the furniture and thus injured my left leg. Therefore, I thought to sit down for some time." Satish held his leg. " It is a belief that if you are going somewhere related to work and your left leg hits an object then you should sit for a while and drink a glass of water before moving forward."

Minnie brought him a glass of water and asked, "do you really believe in this stuff?"

"I don't, but in our bad times we need to believe in it, there is always something behind these beliefs." Satish returned the glass to Minnie.

"I want you to listen to me, I don't feel right sending you alone, my heart is not accepting it, please take Chirag along with you. For my sake." Requested Minnie.

At the very moment, Chirag came downstairs and said, "I could not find anything."

"See, now you cannot say no." Insisted Minnie looking at Satish.

"Chirag, go pack your bags. You have to accompany me for some urgent work. And don't forget your suit." Said Satish.

"We need to go? And Minnie? She would be alone at home." Replied Chirag.

"So what? You do as uncle is saying, I will take care of myself and don't worry, I will call one of my servants, she will be there with me." replied Minnie.

"Ok, uncle. Let's roll." Chirag moved towards his room to pack his belongings. Satish too left for his house and they decided to leave the next day early morning.

Chapter 16

The Unfinished Business

After all hostages arrived at the spot, they were taken to a safe house located underground level 2. Shadow beforehand arranged the setup with his dogs (ROTTWEILER) held by the guards and made the hostages stand in the center. He welcomed the hostages in a sarcastic tone and asked his men to take off the blindfold of all the hostages.

Shankar asked, "where are we brought? Who are you and what do you want from us?"

"Hold your horses and be my guest. Here, only I am allowed to speak and if you talk too much then I will have to feed you to my pets." Shadow laughed.

Shadow then instructed his man to turn the lights on. As the lights were switched on, the dogs started barking at the hostages and were jumping to tear them off. All the hostages were afraid to see the set up.

"Welcome to my safe house where you will be safe only till your dear kids follow my instructions. Don't worry, we shall take care of your essentials, but my only request is don't dare to escape or plan any stupidity, you will get yourself killed." Shadow asked the guards to leave the place and secure them from the outside. All the hostages were waiting for a miracle to happen so that they could escape the place. Meanwhile Shankar was looking around if he could find any loophole, but whenever he touched the wall alarm rang.

The Next day

Both Satish and Chirag left for the place where Satish and Shankar used to work together and lived for many years. After few hours, they reached the destination. He was terrified by seeing the place and murmured, "everything's changed."

A few people were seen walking on the streets with a few vehicles moving around. They stopped their car and parked it in front of a closed shop. As they both got down, they walked towards another car, Chirag said, "uncle see the sticker on this car."

'Permit valid. Expires in ten days from registration.'

"Yesterday was the expiry date." said Satish and called a man who was walking towards the shop. The man saw but ignored him. Satish was blank to see something like that. Both then moved towards the shop. The shopkeeper was an old man aged around 60 years.

"What is all this permit." Asked Satish.

"After the evil woke up, he messed up the state and took the control in his hands by making us his slaves." Replied the man crying.

"What? Salves? Who is the evil?" questioned Satish in fear.

"The evil Krum. If anyone needs to go out of the house, he needs permission and submit all details. Only after approval he or she can move out. If permission is not granted and even the man is dying, he would rather die but not go out. Because if found roaming without a permit, then that person will be taken to the arena and will be thrown in front of Hungry Aliens." Replied the shopkeeper.

"Whoa, it's like a nightmare, and did you say hungry aliens?" asked Chirag. The shopkeeper nodded and looked down.

"Krum? When did he wake up? He was in coma, right?" said Satish.

"You know Krum?" The shopkeeper looked closely and said, "you look familiar to me, are you, Shankar?

"No, I am Satish, the brother of Shankar the great scientist and he is Chirag, Shankar's Son." Satish kept his hand on Chirag's shoulder.

The shopkeeper then held both their hands and pulled them inside his shop. He took them in a room and asked his son to take care of the shop. He then closed the door from the inside. He hugged Satish and said, “where did you people go?”

“What happened here? Tell me everything.” requested Satish

“What is happening, first the hungry aliens and now this, can anyone explain something to me as well?” Chirag sat down.

The old man started narrating the story;

The year was 2010, all of us were celebrating the New Year eve. However, we did not know that it was our last day of celebration, because that day the Evil Krum woke up shouting “I will not spare you Shankar.”

The news went to Zexox the next second after he woke up. Zexox came in his Spaceship and landed on a empty land. Krum’s all men went to receive Zexox in their car, and he brought some gift which was so huge that especially a truck was sent to carry it. Zexox and Krum had a meeting, the details about which were shared with us by some people working there, and the meeting continued about the condition of Krum.

Zexox said, “Krum, now you finally woke up and I was waiting for this moment to come.”

“Let’s go and get Shankar.” said Krum.

“Are you out of your mind? Keep your anger inside, we need to form a base of army here and create an arena, later we shall get Shankar.” replied Zexox.

It's said that some evil power woke him up by giving him powers from which he could rule the place and make us his slaves. Krum's men kidnapped the officials one by one and left them in the arena as a feast to the hungry aliens (gift of Zexox).

The Hungry aliens were specially created for the arena. It's said that the hungry aliens have five eyes, sharp teeth, a slim body, four hands, their each finger has sharp nails which can tear anyone apart and two legs which help them run very fast that no human can compete them. The government also got fed up and could not do anything as government officials escaped the city and the ones who could not escape were killed. After a few days, an election was organized by the chairman of the Sate, under the pressure of Krum. Krum sat on the throne even after he did not get a single vote. He immediately built a huge wall surrounding the city with huge entrance gates that open only on his command. He made all amendments to the rules and punishments that no one could survive in front of him. He also compels us pay double tax which if not paid then the property goes under Krum and his men take the charge of it. That day, if Shankar could have killed him, we could have not seen this day. Anyway, why did you come back and how did you enter the city? I heard that the borders are sealed for out comers and only Krum or his men can come in or move out. Either you are very lucky or Krum's men have trapped you, and thus I cannot let you go out, you will be sent to the arena if found.

Chirag and Satish were listening to the man in grave tension.

"Let's clear the mess and make Krum as our slave, uncle." Said Chirag.

"It's not as easy as you say, son." Replied the old man.

"Now what am I supposed to do? How to find the device to contact JOI? I need to go to Shankar's home, where the lab is in the basement, and search for the device." Satish sat down helplessly.

The man said, "it's impossible for us to even think of it. At night, the situation turns worse, all hungry Aliens are tied to a monster truck, and patrolling is done, if they sniff anyone then that person is gone."

"Please help me out, Shankar and our other sources have been kidnapped by Shadow, the friend of Zexox. We need that device so that JOI can help us to defeat all the enemies." Said Satish folding his hand in front of the man.

"There is one way, but you will have to hide in this place and you cannot move out. If you agree, then only I will tell you the option." Said the Shopkeeper.

Satish nodded in fear and said, "please make it possible and I will do whatever you say."

The Shopkeeper asked for the address and replied after hearing the same, "this building is just three blocks before my home, I daily pass by it while going back home. It seems to be your lucky day and your brother has done many good things for us, therefore this blessing is turning up, or else it would have not been possible."

The shopkeeper then decided to help and made a full proof plan. "Today you will have to stay inside my shop, all food and shelter will be provided to you, but I am strictly warning you, do not make any kind of noise or plan any stupidity. My son and I will move towards home and I will go inside this home and open the lab while my son will reach home. I will search for the device, after finding which I will return home. While coming to shop the next day, I will deliver you the parcel and then my son will be ready with the pass for your vehicle along with the pass for his vehicle which would be going towards his in-laws home. Their home is very near to the border. The in-laws have been staying there for a long time and have dig an underground way from their basement to the opposite side of the border. After you reach the basement; you can drive and escape the city and my son will come back to the in-laws house. Later you come with Shankar and save us from Krum. I know only Shankar can defeat this evil. But remember, if any of Krum's men ask you anything just say that you are a supplier of grains and have come here to deliver the goods as the lorry driver was not delivering in this area. Never look in their eyes and always keep your head down while talking."

Satish was scared and murmured, "I took the right decision by bringing Chirag along." Chirag on other hand was completely clueless about everything. Satish then described the device and gave the man the lab keys. He described the place where the device could be and also a bag to carry it. "Please try to bring all possible parts so that we can connect to JOI."

The shopkeeper took the car details and sent the same to his son for permit pass. He arranged all supplies for them and then left the room and closed the door from the outside. He went on the counter and waited to go home. As it was time, the shopkeeper and his son acted normal, they closed the shop and moved towards home in their car.

Chirag then looked at Satish and asked "do I need to ask further? And can we trust this guy?"

"Fingers crossed, if not, you are here to take care. Your mom and dad would have told you, if I am not wrong, you all even went to the place where you were born, right?" asked Satish.

"Yes, I remember, but that place was outside the city. They told me about the situation; how they managed to escape from the enemies and how I was born hiding from everyone but they did not tell me any names." Replied Chirag.

"Is it so?" Chirag nodded. "Ok, then let them come home, they will explain it in a better way than me. For now, in short, Krum is your dad's biggest enemy and if he finds us, we are gone." explained Satish.

"Hmmm… ok, now what shall we do? I need to see your old home as well." Said Chirag.

"You heard the old man, right? We cannot step out, it's dangerous for us." Said Satish.

"He said it because he did not know about me. I will come back soon, I promise." requested Chirag.

"And what if the guards come in your absence? Dear, I don't think it's the right time for you to step out. I am sorry, I am a guardian responsible for you and we are already in trouble, do you need more?" Replied Satish.

"Ok, uncle. Now don't get emotional. I am not going anywhere, happy?" Chirag smiled.

"It's good to be safe rather than getting in any trouble. Good night, I am sleeping." Satish slept on the bed.

Chapter 17

The Device

As the old man and his son were moving towards their home in the car, they saw Krum's men patrolling in the area as an unknown vehicle had entered the city without permission. The old man's son asked him not to go in search as the situation was not good and he might get killed.

"You were very small and I know how much Shankar and his family had done for our city, so for that sake I will go. You stop the car now. I will walk towards the street and enter the lab from the back gate. You go home and if anyone comes asking for me, say that I am in garage searching for old stuff and send a message on my mobile. I will come home hiding. Keep our back door open so that I can enter quietly." Replied the old man.

The old man walked to the left street and opened the back door to step inside the house. As he entered, it was all black and thus he turned his torchlight on and went in search of the lab. He was finding it quite difficult because everything was covered in dust and was messed up. He managed to reach the lab and began searching for the device as described. Searching in every corner took almost half the night, the old man was tired and found nothing. He was disappointed and walked in another room and sat on a chair looking around. To his surprise, he saw a door in the corner and moved towards it. As he opened it, he found a way downstairs and then reached underground. He saw it was an empty space and nothing was sighted. After observing the place, he found a secret door covered with a curtain. He tried to open the door with full force but it was jammed, so he took some rest and again tried to open the door. He finally managed to open it, but it made a sound while opening.

A guard heard the sound and came inside the house searching if anyone was inside. The old man heard that someone was searching for him so he slowly went up and closed the door wisely. He texted his son to be present outside the house in the morning. He then slept in a corner with the device on his chest and covered himself with a cloth. The guard was fully drunk so he thought it would be his imagination and therefore closed the door and went away. The next day, the old man woke up and silently reached outside the house and locked it. He then saw his son waiting for him and both moved towards the shop.

The old man gave Satish the device and said, "our work is done, so you go now before anyone comes in search of you." The drunk guard became fresh in the morning and updated his boss about the night's incident. The boss became mad and slapped the guard, not because he was drunk but because it was Krum's strict order to intimate any movement seen or heard in the lab as it was Shankar's lab. The boss kicked him and said, "people like you should be thrown in the arena for being careless." He then ran towards the lab with the guard and saw the lock. The drunk guard said, "I swear I opened it and went inside." The boss took a close look and said, "You're right, as the lock is clean without any dust on it."

Immediately through a radio, the information was shared to the main building and the boss said, "emergency, send the dogs for sniffing." Alien Dogs were sent and a few more guards came and started searching the lab. They then followed the footprints but they did not find anything. The dog managed to sense the old man's smell and pulled the guards to his the shop and stopped. The guard asked, "where did you go last night?"

"Where will I go? I am already tired of my age." Replied the old man coughing.

The Guard said, "let me know if you find anything" and went off. However, he sensed some doubt and decided to keep and eye on the shop for a few days.

The old man's son left with Chirag and Satish before the guard came. Before leaving the state, Satish thanked the old man's son and successfully crossed the border.

Satish and Chirag reached home safely from the dangerous place. The servant opened the door as they came. Satish saw the whole house was cleaned and kept fresh. He appreciated the servant and then both Chirag and Satish went in the lab and gave the device to Minnie.

"Here it is. Try if you can fix this." Said Satish and sat on the chair next to Minnie.

Chirag told everything to Minnie and sat near her as he too was very tired.

"Don't worry. Let our dad come, we shall get all the details and yes, I will fix it but for our first task we would not need JOI." Replied Minnie.

She then asked both to follow her outside.

Chapter 18

Task 1

They all sat in the living room and Minnie started to explain the plan.

"I have found the place 'The Historic House.' It is very secured, army officials are being appointed for the security because it has many objects which can be stolen from our neighboring country. Those objects are historic and many countries have eyes on them. Entering inside is only possible if we have a permission taken six months before, and after taking the permission, a guy will be assigned to us and will have a watch on us. Only a group of five people enter at a time. Before entering, we need to change our clothes to the ones given by them. Non-living objects can be taken inside. The best part is that the place is secured only from the outside, whereas from the inside everything is fake because when I checked the company name I could not find any such. I think the device is set to scare people; once anyone enters the device on the door, it will scan the person from top to bottom and if anything dangerous is found according to the device then the laser rays will split the person into two. So this is how a person can enter the Museum."

Satish and Chirag kept listening to her quietly.

"I have contacted a source who is into fake passports field. He will give us six passports; two for each of each of us. One to go from Inland to the Green world and other identity from Green world to Inland. For the first identity, we need to kidnap three suspects or make the targets miss the trip who have taken permission. They are going with a group of people across Inland and meeting at one point to start the trip to Green world together with the help of tours and travelers. So I have selected three different persons who suit our requirement and we will have to make them miss the journey by kidnapping them or as you people suggest. Next, we will be given the details, descriptions and Dimensions of the objects present in museum by our tour guide. Uncle, you have to remember the size of 'the mirror of Queen Alice W/o King. Andrew' and purchase the same size of the mirror and give it to Chirag who will resize and make the object small and hide it in the uniform. And Chirag, you need to make a gadget(cameo) which can deactivate all camera recordings and all to be set on a timer. When the final time will come, all the cameras should go off and the electricity should be cut. I will become invisible and we both will move towards the original mirror. You will give me the fake object and then wait outside to see if any guard comes towards me and inform me the same. I will till then make the real mirror disappear and replace it with the duplicate one. Before the electricity turns on again, we three shall join the squad and go towards the exit point. I will then take the gadget (cameo) and the original mirror and meet you at the airport directly. Subsequently, we all three will reach home waiting for the first person to be released."

Chirag and Satish clapped for the plan made by Minnie as it was indeed fabulous.

"Yes, in this manner no one could identify if the original mirror is missing." Chirag smiled. "Well, I have a question, if I hide the object in the uniform then the device on the door would identify the same."

"No, don't worry. The scanner won't be able to identify your object as many other small objects would be present in your uniform like chain and buttons so it will not scan the mirror."

"Perfect, madam. And how are we taking the gadget inside, you have not mentioned that in the plan?"

"Good question. So, for that, you need to make a small bee which would work on your instruction as it will have artificial intelligence devised in it. Alter the gadget in a small size and add a small button which can be pressed by the bee's sting. First, while you change the dress, you will activate the bee and fly it to the Museum and instruct it to hide behind the first description paper. When you enter the museum, take the bee and keep it in your hand. Press the button when you feel is the right time to and thus the cameras will be switched off and the electricity will be cut.

Also make night vision lenses to see in the dark as once the electricity goes off, all the doors will be shut and everything will be dark."

"Ok, noted." Replied Chirag.

"Minnie, how about the three people we will kidnap? Won't they confess the truth later?" Asked Satish.

"Those three will be given an injection with a different type of anesthesia liquid prepared by me. It is capable to play with the brains and do a chemical reaction on the membrane. Whatever we will ask them to speak will be fixed in their brain cells for 30 days and they will repeat the same when asked about it. They will forget everything about the event and continue their normal life and when asked about the trip, they will say it was fun.

All three promised each other that they would not harm or kill anyone on this mission and everything will be done like a professional. They decided that if anyone got caught, the other two members will have to leave and after completing the mission they will come back to help and till then try to stay alive. Minnie had a word with his agent for tickets and they started to pack their bags. They all had only thirty hours for the trip so they needed to hurry.

The three targets

After 30 hours:

All three hugged each other and moved towards their targets. They went in different directions; Chirag went in the South, Minnie went to the West and Satish went to the East.

Minnie's target was a lady of age 26 named Lilly martin; she was alone in this world with limited contacts and grew up as an orphan. Lilly used to work in a company as a clerk. Her only dream was to see the Mirror which the queen used to admire so she wanted to go on this trip. It was very easy for Minnie to tackle her. Minnie reached the destination and went to the victim's house being invisible. She banged the door three times. Lilly was in the kitchen and as she heard the sound, she went towards the door shouting, "hold on. I am coming." She opened the door but found no one there. She then murmured, "it might be the naughty children" and closed the door. In that gap, Minnie entered the house and sat on the slab of the kitchen. As Lilly went to the kitchen, Minnie took the opportunity and injected her while whispering in her ears, "the trip was amazing and I finally saw the mirror." She covered the lady's mouth with a handkerchief by adding chloroform on it and made her unconscious. The dose was high enough to let her stay unconscious for the next 24 hours. Minnie carried Lilly and made her sleep in the bedroom and then she turned normal and took Lilly's phone and transferred all details of the trip. Next, she dressed like Lilly and acted as if she was leaving for the trip and locked the main door. Then Minnie moved towards the airport by completing her job and reached home safely. She decided to gift Lilly the mirror's photo and a free trip voucher for ten days.

Chirag's target was a little difficult to manage. The guy named Ted, aged 30 years old who had a famous gym in the city. He got the tickets for the trip in a lucky draw and even if he missed the trip he did not care. Chirag decided to make him unconscious in his Gym and put a notice outside stating, 'under maintenance.' Chirag reached the destination and moved towards the target and waited for all to disperse so that he could take him down. Till then Chirag purchased a local brand liquor bottle and waited downstairs. Chirag then saw the time was 9 pm and realized that he had only one hour to leave for the airport. At 9.15 pm, when all the gym members dispersed, Chirag with the help of the gadget turned all the cameras off and covered his face and entered the gym. He saw that the guy was alone and sitting with the air pods listening high music. Chirag slowly moved towards him and injected him while whispering in his ears, "the trip was amazing and I enjoyed a lot." Next, Chirag covered Ted's mouth with a handkerchief which had Chloroform on it and the dose was normal so that he could get up the next day around 8 pm. Chirag opened his bag and took out the alcohol bottle and sprayed the alcohol on Ted's dress. He took Ted's phone and transferred all the trip's details and moved towards the desk and wrote a note in big letters, 'Gym Closed. Under Maintenance.' Chirag locked the gym door from the outside and left for the airport.

Satish's target was a difficult one named Mathew, age 42, a history teacher. He had a wife and two children and lived in a small apartment. He was so addicted to historic places that he had sent his folder in a contest organized by the Museum authorities and had won the contest. As a prize, he was given an opportunity to visit the Museum, but the problem was that only he could go on the trip and not his family. Her wife was mad at him plus they did not have enough money to afford the trip. Satish was not willing to leave the man unconscious at any place as he had a family. Satish reached the destination and went towards Mathew's Apartment and waited outside. He called Minnie and asked, "how am I going to do this? I cannot stop him by making him unconscious, so shall we kidnap him?"

"Wait, let me check the tours and travelers pick up point, till then wait for my call and observe the guy." Minnie searched the pickup point on her laptop.

Minnie then called Satish and said, "the pickup point is very far and we cannot do anything. Try to crack the deal by offering him double the price and take the voucher in return."

"Now that's a marvelous idea." replied Satish and disconnected the call.

Satish went to Mathew's home and registered himself as a tour agent in the apartment register. As he rang the bell, Mathew opened the door and asked, "yes, how can I help you?"

"I am Anand from the tours and traveler's agency. You have a tour to the Green world, right?" Replied Satish.

"Yes, tell me?" questioned Mathew.

"I need to discuss a deal with you." Satish held his bag close to himself.

"Ok, come in." Mathew made him sit on the couch and offered some tea.

"Sir, have you packed your bags for the trip?" asked Satish.

Mathew's wife was listening to everything from the kitchen and replied in anger, "no need to go on any trip or else I will leave this home." Mathew heard his wife and replied in embarrassment, "I have not yet packed and am still in a dilemma whether to go or not."

Satish then requested Mathew to call his wife and told her as she arrived, "madam, I have an offer for you both."

Mathew's wife ran towards Satish and asked, "what offer, sir? Is it for the whole family? Are we going to get a new TV?"

"Madam, please sit first. I will explain everything." Satish smiled. "Sir and madam, our travel agency has decided to gift you a holiday package for 2+2 members for 8 days in a hill station with a luxurious stay. If you are interested, then you need to return the voucher of Green world trip and this hill station trip tickets will be given for free with no additional cost for stay."

Hearing this, Mathew's wife started dancing with happiness whereas Mathew stood like a nerd as if he was not at all interested.

Mathew's wife hurried to her bedroom and brought the voucher. She handed it to Satish and said, "thank you, sir."

Satish was surprised that Mathew stood still and did not utter a word.

"Sir, please go. Go, go, before he changes his mind." Said Mathew's wife.

Satish then got up thanking them and went out of the building. He took a cab and reached the airport to return home.

All three got united at home and celebrated happily. They packed their bags and moved towards the pickup point. After reaching, they behaved as strangers and started the trip. All three acted as if becoming friends with each other and started to share their lunch and laughed together discussing their life story.

Satish read the manual and saw the mirror dimensions. When they reached Green world, he went to the market in search of the mirror. It was obvious that if a place has a special item then it would be available in the black too. Satish found the similar piece and purchased the same. He did the payment and asked the shopkeeper to deliver it to the hotel along with him. He then went to the hotel and the delivery man placed the mirror on the bed.

As the delivery man left, Satish called Chirag. As soon as Chirag entered the room, Satish locked the door from the inside. "Perfect," uttered Chirag after seeing himself in the mirror. Next, he flipped his bag to the front and took out the secret gadget of his dad. Flashing the same, he reduced the mirror's size equivalent to a small button and kept it carefully in his bag.

Chapter 19

The Museum

The Next morning, everyone got ready and started the journey towards the Museum in a van. Everyone was singing and playing, and reached the Museum enjoying the journey. The van was parked in the parking area and everyone started to move towards the counter for verification. Minnie saw that it was a big line, so asked Chirag to set up the gadget and set a timer of one hour.

As everyone moved forward slowly, Chirag grabbed the opportunity and casually moved towards the security room. The guards were spread everywhere as that day unexpectedly many people came to visit. So, the army people were busy handling the crowd. Thus, Chirag managed to get inside and stuck a gadget which would turn off the lights and cameras after one hour. As he was moving out after setting up, an army officer came and him.

"What are you doing near the security room?" questioned the Officer.

“I was just hanging around and looking for the washroom.” Replied Chirag casually.

“Hmmm, better stay away or I will sue you,” warned the Officer and noted all the details of Chirag on a paper and kept it in his pocket. The officer then moved towards the main gate. Chirag went to Minnie and asked, “now what, he got all my details?”

“Don’t worry, I will bring the paper from his pocket. You stand in the cue and wait for our turn.” Minnie went behind the security room and became invisible. She went towards the army officer and tapped his shoulder from the back. The officer turned back and said in anger, “how many times I have told you not to call me from back.” He was surprised to see no one standing and Minnie silently took out the paper from his pocket and hid it. The army officer was shocked and moved away.

Minnie then became visible and whispered to herself, “so damn easy.” She joined the line with Chirag. At the moment, an announcement was made, “those without permission are requested to leave the area and those with permission, please move towards the check-in.” All unwanted people left the place and people with permission went on the verification desk. As they verified themselves, they were sent to the changing room according to their batch allotted. Minnie, Chirag and Satish were luckily in the same batch. Chirag silently activated the bee carrying the gadget and set it to fly and hide behind the first object description chart. Next, they changed their dresses and Chirag hid the mirror in a way that it does not fall off.

Everyone got ready and were waiting for their turn to see the mirror.

When their turn came, all the five people entered the scanner one by one and Chirag was the last to enter. As he stepped in, the lights started blinking suddenly. All the army officials panicked and couldn't asses as to what happened. Chirag took the opportunity and quickly skipped the scanner and entered without getting scanned.

Near the first object, the supervisor was explaining the session and Chirag acted to faint. He acted to get up with the support of the description table and silently took the bee in hand and covered it. The Supervisor and all others started laughing at him. As they moved forward, they saw the Mirror was kept in an open place. Minnie whispered in Chirag's ear "change in the plan. You take the charge because the position is changed."

All three looked at each other and showed a thumbs-up indicating 'easy job.' Everyone moved forward and went near the Mirror. At the moment, Chirag's Cameo gadget timer ended and the power was cut along with the cameras being deactivated. It was completely dark and the supervisor said, "everyone, freeze on your positions and if found guilty, you will be shot on the spot."

"With the help of the special lenses in his eyes, Chirag managed to reach near the mirror. He took out the fake mirror and turned it huge with the help of the bee's sting. Next, he turned the original mirror in a button size object and kept it inside. He placed the duplicate mirror in place and made the gadget small and attached it to the bee which he hid in hand. He silently returned to him team.

In a few minutes, the current came back and the supervisor analyzed if everyone was in their position. The task was done so smoothly that no one doubted them. They quietly moved towards the exit and went to change their dress. Next, they sat in the van and moved towards the hotel. As soon as they reached the hotel, all three packed their bags and left a note which read, 'we are extending the tour. Do not wait for us and move forward. Thank you.'

They managed to reach the Inland airport and Minnie then took the cube in hand and pressed the symbol followed by typing the code. In a few seconds, a location was sent in the cube and as it was on the way to their home, they decided to book two cabs. In one, Minnie went to the location and submitted the mirror and on the other, Chirag and Satish headed home. As per the plan, all three reached home and were waiting excited to meet the first person.

Chapter 20

Shadow is Everywhere

On the very same of Minnie submitting the mirror, as all the hostages got up in the morning, all facilities were given and before they got up the food was ready on the table. All hostages sat together and had their breakfast. Suddenly, the door opened and five guards and a dog moved towards them.

"Good morning, hope you all had a good sleep. Well, I have a small surprise for you." Said Shadow as he entered behind his men.

A guard moved towards the wall and turned the TV on. A video was then played which displayed all the movements in the museum. Shankar shouted, "what is all this and why are you putting my kids in danger? What do you want?"

"I want to be a powerful person and make you all my slaves." Shadow started laughing.

"Then do it at your will and not on others." Replied Shankar in a heavy voice.

Shadow ignored him and said pointing towards his guards, "what are you still waiting for? Go and fetch that girl."

The guards went towards Minnie's friend and dragged her out of the room. Shankar was trying not to let her go but the dog came in between and he had no option but to let her go.

"Where the hell are you taking her?" questioned Shankar.

"How can I spoil the surprise? Wait for your turn and you will know it. Till then, take care of others." Replied Shadow.

Shadow then went to the place where the mirror was kept and scanned it to check if any transmitter was hidden. He safely kept it in a position facing diagonal, and decided to set Minnie's friend free as she was too irritating.

Back at Mi-Chi's place, Satish asked Minnie, "how was the place you visited?"

"I got out from the cab and entered the home. I saw no one was there, so I went backside and when I opened the door, I saw an empty land. I walked further and further but no one was sighted. Suddenly, I heard an engine sound but saw nothing. As I faced up, I saw a chopper right above me. A big box was coming down from it with a rope attached and it landed near me. I opened the box and kept the mirror in it and closed the door. The box was pulled up and the door closed and flew away. I could not see anyone." She took out the cube and kept it on the table and asked, "shall I press the number two, as our first task is done and we have five more to complete?"

Satish and Chirag nodded in agreement.

Minnie then pressed the number two and the cube pieces again started to change their positions. The numbers went backside and a small cube box opened with a paper coming out. Minnie took the paper out and the screen flashed with a note which stated, "we appreciate your work, you stole the mirror so well that no one could identify it and your gift is on its way. I know you are very smart Minnie, so start planning for the next assignment and don't do anything stupid or else all your loved once will be killed."

After seeing the message, Chirag got an idea and said, "After we complete the next task, we will hide a transmitter in the object so that we get to know the place where the objects are being taken."

"It's not as easy as you say. The object gets scanned before being pulled." Replied Minnie.

"How can you be so sure?" asked Chirag.

"I saw a ray of red light scanning the object while it was being pulled. Anyway, your idea is good. We will plan something about it, your bee can help us."

"How did Shadow know about our plan, was he around us, or was he with us?" asked Satish.

Minnie listened carefully and replied, "oh gosh, how can we be so stupid." Minnie sat on the couch. "He was with us all the time. How did so many people enter even after knowing that the Museum takes appointment before six months. And the two people standing in front of me were talking about some free entry voucher, when I was about to ask them, suddenly an Army officer came and caught Chirag which distracted my attention. He acted to write down Chirag's details because when I saw the paper, it was blank. Shadow first took the form of an Army officer."

"Impressive, huh." Said Chirag raising his eyebrows.

"Then he took the form of our supervisor and moved along with us." Continued Minnie.

"How can you be so sure that he was the supervisor?" questioned Chirag.

"What do you think, when you escaped the main door no one saw you?" Minnie smirked. "I noticed that the supervisor saw you, but when I looked at him, he acted by looking here and there. The gadget which you hid in the security room was missing when I went to take it back. I never told you about it but when I went to handover the Mirror, at the end, when the box was pulled, this gadget dropped from the sky and broke into two pieces."

"Oh my god, it was all planned. And we were thinking that everything was going so smoothly. But why did he do that? And if all the guards were replaced with Shadow's men and if he is capable to replace the army guards then why did he compel us do all this? I mean, he could have done this more smoothly than we did. Why us?" said Chirag.

"Good logic. Even I am thinking the same. But somewhere I think he wanted to know about our capabilities so that he can defeat us with our weakness." replied Minnie.

"How can you manage to do things in a better way and solve everything? If you can be more alert, then we can be one step ahead of him." Chirag smiled.

"I was a bit disturbed so I was not able to focus. Next time, I promise I will search his hub and make sure we reach the hub before we start the third task." replied Minnie.

"Now what has happened is gone. Well, I think you should be known with the face?" asked Satish.

"I am not sure uncle, but if I meet him again, I will surely be able to identify him." Minnie assured. "We have only three more out of country tasks, after that both the tasks are in our country and if we need to reach Shadow early, then we need to make a perfect plan and get him at the earliest. Also, this time, I will be one step ahead of him. Well, it's time to contact JOI." She uncovered the device. "Chirag, I need you to make a few gadgets."

"Yes, tell me." Replied Chirag.

"No.1 – make 10 bees with tiny cameras fit in their eyes, and transmitters on their sting, also the color should be yellow only. Bees should be connected in pairs and each pair should be operated by one remote. The distance from the remote to bees should be two-kilometer radii to operate. And yes, don't forget to put a satellite chip, so that if the bees are far from us we shall operate them by linking it to the satellite and till their battery life runs off. The remotes should show us how far are the bees. Also, make a portable charging box that can be compatible to carry in handbags; this could help us charge the bees.

No.2 – Eye lenses through which we can see in the dark, make at least 5 pairs.

No.3 – Sticky suit for me with a remote switch on the wrist to activate whichever part I need to switch on.

No.4 – Add a laser feature on dad's gadget with an aiming feature. And last,

No.5 - Some small Bluetooth pods from which, if we leave one ear pod at a place and after connecting it internally, we can hear everything at the other EarPods at a 1-kilometer radius. Make 9 additional pieces with one main piece which would be connected to all other.

Satish uncle, please help Chirag in making these devices. I will then have some tasks to complete."

Minnie then went out and drove to her office. While driving, Minnie's friend called Minnie to inform about her return.

Minnie reached her office and instructed her assistant, "all appointments to be called off for next month and if any emergency arises, contact me. Don't call for silly doubts, you can take the call as you are working here for many years and you also have experience in judging a good deal and a bad deal. My business should not be affected in anyway. I will increase your pay and a new home will shortly be given to you." The personal assistant got excited and replied, "Thank you, madam." Minnie replied, "Now stop blushing and help me in my work, sit down." Minnie then made a list of files and recordings needed. She was trying to get any information possible about Shadow. She handed over the paper to the assistant and said, "first, I need you to give a list of the meetings which I and Dhiraj have attended together. Second, I need the recording of the last three meetings from the conference hall. If they refuse to give, try to take it by offering some gifts and even if they don't, then choose the other way. Third, I want the last 10 deals signed by Dhiraj. Fourth, you only have one week to give me all these.

"One week is too less, madam." Replied the assistant looking down.

"You have two options; either do it or I will fire you." Minnie angrily looked at her.

"Ok, madam, I will do it." Replied the assistant.

"Now that's like a good girl." Minnie left the office.

Minnie knew Shadow would have attended at least one meeting and she would surely catch him. Minnie went home and started the device to connect to JOI for his help. Though the device was activated, but still to begin the connection, Shankar's eyes scan was a must. Once scanned, an automatic message would be sent to JOI's computer with a notification 'Shankar's device activated.' Minnie thus decided to hide the device until they get the eyes scanned. She took a paper and began working on plan two.

Chapter 21

Task 2

After two days, Minnie was ready with the second plan. She called Satish and Chirag in the living room and began explaining. "The second task is an easy task. This time, only Chirag and I will be going, whereas uncle, you have to stay here and guide us. We both will reach the place with changed identities and enter the building at night so that we can easily take on the security guards and enter the lab. Chirag will first go to the security room and hide the gadget to deactivate all the cameras, then we both will go to the third floor and take the sunshine device and turn it small. Next, we will replace it with a dummy model and escape the building by taking the gadget from the security room. Is everything clear?"

"And what am I supposed to do at home?" asked Satish.

"Ok, your role will be to safeguard us from the outside if any problem arises. We will use the exit plan and you'll help us execute it." Replied Minnie.

"Yes, it's better that you take me along as I am your lucky charm." Satish smiled.

"Yes, my Lucky Angel." Replied Minnie. Both Mi-Chi laughed.

"Don't forget the bees." Said Minnie.

"Only one pair is ready for now." Replied Chirag.

"Ok, for now, a pair is enough to take along." Minnie smiled.

All three promised each other that they shall not hurt or kill anyone in this mission. After the discussion, all dispersed to their rooms to pack their bags with possible gadgets and changed their appearance. They assembled in the living room after packing and then moved towards the airport.

All three reached the destination around 6pm so they decided not to book any hotel for stay as the estimated time for the completion of the mission was by 1 am. All three went to a restaurant for their dinner. Next, Chirag went out and found a shop named 'Juliet's garage.' He called Satish and asked him to rent a car so that they could make an exit plan if anything went wrong.

Satish entered the store and offered more money for the car and took the car without submitting the documents. All three then travelled through the car to reach the lab. Minnie took a nap in the car, while Satish and Chirag kept wandering and noted all the possible exit points. Chirag then opened a navigation app in his mobile to check which route connected where and made a full proof exit plan.

Pointing towards the mobile screen, Chirag explained, "Uncle, I want you to wait at the corner of this road under that tree and after my signal, you drive in the reverse towards me and we shall leave the place by turning towards the third left and then right after a kilometer. We shall hide our car between these two buildings and we shall exit from the car and sleep as a beggar. When we find the way clear, we will exit the place and take another route towards the airport. After we reach half way, a big dump yard will come on our right so we will hide the car over there and change our dress and take a cab to reach the airport. Minnie will not be with us as she will get invisible and hide herself. She will meet us directly at the airport. I hope you are clear and yes, don't drive slow as you dive in the city, please."

"Huh, I was a racer when I was of your age and cops were never able to catch me." Satish smirked.

"Really?" Chirag laughed.

It was 10 pm and they decided to start the mission at 11.45 pm. Till then all three waited for everyone to disperse from the place and clear the area for them to enter.

It was 11.45pm.

"Let's begin, Chirag. We both will stay together no matter what happens." Minnie held Chirag's hand.

Mi-Chi then enters the lab by jumping from the wall. Minnie got invisible and went near the main guard. She hit on his neck from behind and made him unconscious. Chirag injected the other guards and made them unconscious, Mi-Chi moved towards the main gate and found the cameras on, therefore they hid themselves behind a tree. Minnie entered the lab and went inside the security camera room. She saw two guards looking at the screen monitoring the movements. She hit the first guard on his neck and injected the second guard making them both unconscious. She switched the cameras off and then signaled Chirag to get in. Next, both slowly moved towards the staircase and reached the third floor. Minnie went inside the room and searched for the machine. On the other hand, Chirag went in another room and searched for the machine.

After a few minutes, they both came out and showed a thumbs down to each other. They entered the next room together and began the search. Chirag found the machine and called Minnie to confirm the same. Minnie gestured with a thumbs up and asked Chirag to resize the machine and replace it with a dummy machine. Chirag followed her words and both then left the room. They reached the ground floor by taking the stairs. Minnie heard some sound, so she asked Chirag to hide behind the door. Minnie got invisible and slightly opened the door peeking outside, "Oh my god, how did the cops enter the lab?"

"What? Did you say cops?" asked Chirag in shock.

"I think Shadow is testing us and he would have informed the cops." replied Minnie.

"I am not going to leave him." Replied Chirag in a low tone.

"It's not the time to rage. Control it and do as I say." Said Minnie. "Go on the terrace of the building and try to escape from there and meet uncle. I am glad that you made an exit plan and now it's time to execute it."

"Ok, please take care and reach safely to the airport." Replied Chirag and left the place.

The cops rushed inside the building and saw the guards down. Therefore, the Officer ordered the men to secure the building and begin the search.

All the cops began their search. Minnie was invisible and hid behind the door waiting for the right time to escape. An officer opened the door and entered. He looked behind the door and went upstairs. Minnie went out of the door and exited the building safely.

Chirag reached the terrace and looked around to find an escape. He found a branch of a tree so he climbed on the tree and slowly got down without making noise. An Officer from the first-floor window saw the tree shaking. He closely looked towards it, but did not find anyone. Therefore, he closed the window and turned towards the next room. Chirag saw the officer looking at him, so he hid behind a big branch and waited for the officer to look away. The moment the officer turned, Chirag jumped from the tree and landed on the ground. As he started to run towards Satish, a cop standing on the third-floor balcony saw him running. He shouted, "stop or I will shoot you." He then shot, but the aim was missed. He screamed and informed the other cops that a guy in black suit was running towards the main gate. Chirag till then crossed the main gate and rushed to Satish.

"Exit plan activated." Said Chirag.

Satish started the car and changed its gear like a pro while hitting the accelerator and moved as per the plan. All the cops got down and drove to find the car. Satish drove as the plan and hid the car in the lane between the buildings. They both then went in the opposite direction and pretended to sleep. The cops looked for the car but didn't find anyone as it was late.

Satish whispered to Chirag, "my heart is not allowing me to drive the same car. We can get caught, so let's leave the car and inform the owner about the car being here.

"Then what about the plan?" questioned Chirag.

"I am getting a strong intuition, please listen to me. If we drive the same car, the chances of the cops reaching us are very high as it is late night and no vehicles are on the road at this time. We will surely get caught." Requested Satish.

"Ok, I will change the dress and then let's go." Chirag always kept a spare dress in the bag.

Chirag along with Satish walked towards the main road. As they exited the lane, they were shocked to see cops blocking the main road. The cops were searching every vehicle that passed. Chirag and Satish both acted like drunkards and walked towards the road. They passed the cops and managed to reach the main road. The cops did not bother even after seeing them and ignored their presence. Chirag and Satish moved a little forward and took a cab to reach the airport. The cab driver did not say anything because he saw the cops. Therefore, he turned the meter down and moved towards the opposite side.

Chirag looked at Satish and said in a low tone, "you saved us today. How do you get so strong intuitions?" Chirag then asked the driver to drive to the airport.

"When we walk on the right path and if our intentions are right then nothing bad can happen to us." Replied Satish. They both reached the airport and waited for Minnie.

In the meantime, Minnie silently moved towards the street and hid behind a gate. From a distance, she saw a local gang of five people irritating a cab driver. She turned invisible and ran towards the gang. She screamed loudly and the gang got frightened. The gang members looked around and ran away. Minnie laughed and turned normal. She sat in the cab asking the driver to move towards the airport. The cab driver asked, "How did you do that?"

"Who said I did that?" Minnie giggled.

"I think this place is haunted, I will never come to this place again." The cab driver drove her to the airport.

Minnie reached the airport and saw Satish and Chirag waiting for her.

"How did you manage to escape? Anyway, good plan, Chirag." Minnie smiled.

"No, all thanks to uncle." Replied Chirag and explained everything to Minnie.

"Oh, great job uncle." Minnie smiled warmly. "Chirag, you did the right thing by following your elders."

The police tried every possible way to track them but never found any evidence. When they searched the lab, they found everything normal and according to them nothing was missing. The cops thought that the robber would have seen them and so he escaped without taking anything. They all laughed and closed the case.

All three boarded the flight and reached to their city. Minnie then went to hand over the cube and the rest two left for home.

She took out the cube and entered the details. A location popped up. The location was very far from the airport and it took an hour to reach. As she reached there, she saw a port and quietly went inside. She reached near the edge and waited with the bees hidden under the sleeves. An automatic chopper arrived above her; the door opened and a wooden crate came down. Minnie put the machine inside and made it huge with the help of the gadget. The wooden crate was pulled up and the door was about to close. Minnie then threw the bees before the chopper could exit. At the same time, with the remote, she guided another pair and made it land on the aircraft. Albeit the bee landed on the chopper, but as the chopper began to move, one bee fell off in the water. The another bee luckily was stuck in the corner gap of the door. Minnie noticed the same and then went towards home.

Chapter 22
The Bees

All the hostages were sleeping and suddenly an alarm rang. Hearing that, all the hostages woke up and checked if everyone was at their place. The officer asked, "did anyone try to dig around?" The other hostages replied with a no.

"It might be the evil who has disturbed us, and I think it's time for his next target." The guards entered the place with a dog and waited for the instructions.

Shadow entered. "Sorry, folks. I disturbed you, but I cannot wait more to surprise you and so, here I am." Shadow laughed.

"You piece of crap. Why are you hiding behind the wall? If you have guts then face me man to man." Shouted Shankar

"Don't worry, my friend. I have also planned that, but not so soon. Come on, don't spoil the plan." Shadow gestured his guard who then went near the TV and showed them a video. In the video, Chirag was running and a cop was firing at him. The guard stopped the video. Shadow laughed and said, "well, I informed the cops about the lab and see the boy is talented, no doubt in it, but unfortunately…" Shadow laughed.

"No, please. No." Screamed Swati.

"Wait, you stupid lady. I have not completed yet. So, he managed to escape, but I promise you that I will kill him in front of your eyes." Said Shadow in a heavy voice.

"The joke was nice, but you will see some twists in the game." Shankar smiled with a hope kindled in his heart.

"You think your kids will defeat me? If you do, you are badly mistaken as that is never going to happen. I have plans for them in the next task and I will make sure that it would be your kids last task." Shadow laughed.

"Let's see what happens and wait for time to reveal." Replied Shankar.

"Guards, fetch the boy. I am waiting outside." Shadow moved out of the room.

This time, Shankar managed to come in between." The guards moved towards Chirag's friend and dragged him out. Chirag's friend kept screaming and asked for help, but it was not possible as the dog was very dangerous.

Back at Minnie's place, all three gathered in the lab around 8pm and started to discuss if they missed anything.

Minnie told them that one bee safely landed on the aircraft. She took the remote and asked Chirag to track it. In the meantime, she went and brought the device to contact JOI.

"What about the eye scanning?" Asked Satish.

"The bee has quite good camera lenses, clear enough to scan dad's eyes" replied Minnie.

"Let's try, fingers crossed" Satish smiled.

Chirag activated the remote; it displayed one bee's status was disconnected and another bee was approximately 8000 kilometers away. "How are we going to move the bee, we are so far away?

"This was the reason I asked you to link it with the computer so that we can operate it with the help of satellite rays. Understood?" replied Minnie.

"What a genius you are." Chirag hugged Minnie.

"Ok. Now go and turn on the computer. I will link the bee with the satellite and try to operate it." replied Minnie.

It took Minnie around one hour to link the bee. She got up and asked Chirag to move the bee with the remote. Chirag tried to move the bee, but since it was stuck in the corner gap of the door, it would have moved only when then door opened. All three kept waiting for the door to open. After a few hours, Minnie told Satish and Chirag to keep an eye on it while she would get the next list from the cube.

The next morning, the door opened and Chirag suddenly woke up. He saw some movements on the screen and thus observed closely. A group of men were moving towards the chopper carrying Chirag's friend. He then operated the bee and made it fly in the sky to make it reach the maximum height. He looked around and saw full greenery; he analyzed the place as a forest. He slowly moved the bee inside the warehouse and made it sit on a guard's helmet. The guard was safeguarding the place and moved inside out.

After a few minutes, the guard pressed a code on the door and went inside the warehouse. The guard moved forward and stood near the lift. The gate opened and he pressed the button L2 and the lift started to move down. It opened from another side and then the guard reached the lab section. He met the main doctor and had a small conversation.

As he moved towards the next door, he entered another code and went inside a room which had a big glass partition door in between. On the other side of the glass were the hostages; the hostages couldn't see the guard but the guard could see the hostages. Chirag saw the set up and it seemed like a home; all the facilities were provided. Suddenly, he saw his mom, dad, Anu aunty, Raman uncle and the police officer sitting on a dining table discussing something. Shankar had a bandage on his head and all five held each other's hands and were praying. The guard turned around and moved towards the lift.

Battery life 10%.

Chirag flew the bee away and looked for a way to reach Shankar.

Battery life 8%

He saw the battery level and said, "oh no, I need to scan dad's eyes." Thankfully, he found an air blower which was connected to the room. He flew the bee inside it and directed it out from the other end. The bee entered the room and was directed slowly towards Shankar. Chirag woke up Satish and asked him to turn on the device as he was near Shankar. Satish got up and brought the device; he logged in and turned it towards the computer screen. As soon as the bee reached towards Shankar, he just opened his eyes and the bee fell.

Battery Dead

"Oh no. We were so close." Chirag hit the remote.

Satish kept the device aside and sat disappointingly.

beep beep beep beep.

"The sound is coming from the device." Exclaimed Satish.

"Yes, we did it. Minnie's plan worked." Said Chirag. He got up danced with happiness.

"By the way, where is Minnie, we need to inform her?" asked Satish. He searched for her, but she was missing.

Chirag called her but she didn't receive. "She might be sleeping."

"Yes, maybe. Ok, let's wait for her, till then we should send a message to JOI." Replied Satish.

Satish took the device and saw a page displaying a message, 'before you start typing, you need to read our language.' Satish only read how to type 'Shankar kidnapped, need help' with the letters pattern mentioned on the page. He typed the same on the keyboard and pressed the send button. There was no response from JOI. He again sent the same three times, but there was no response at all. He then kept the device on the table and asked Chirag to have breakfast first. As both sat on the dining table, Minnie entered home.

"Device activated." Exclaimed Chirag.

Minnie replied in excitement, "really? Great work guys." She hugged both of them and sat along for breakfast.

At Shadows place

All the five people in the room were looking at the bee. Shankar took the bee in hand and observed it closely. He said in a low tone, "our kids found us."

Everyone had a bright smile on their faces.

Shankar hid the bee in his hand and said, "Swati, I think its charge is over, and I believe I know how to charge it. For now, let's not celebrate and hide this." Everyone nodded their heads in agreement.

Back at Minnie's place, Minnie asked Chirag, "did you find out the location?"

Chirag told her everything.

"It's ok. Next time we shall be fully prepared." Replied Minnie.

Chirag got a call from his friend. "Hey, thank you so much. I reached home safely, and thank you for the efforts."

"It's ok, how's my mom and dad?" asked Chirag.

"All ok, but you need to hurry. We didn't know where we were taken and I think I have reached from that place to my home in 12hrs, so that place might be far enough, and I am sorry I could not fetch more details." Said Chirag's friend.

"It's ok. You take care of yourself. I will soon find them, you get ready and spend some time with family and wait for my call, I may need your help" replied Chirag.

Minnie's assistant gave all the relevant files to Minnie and apologized for the delay. Minnie checked all the files one by one; first she checked the list of people who attended the meeting, but she could not find any name as Shadow, people from all over the world were in the meeting. Next, she played all the videos one by one, in every Video Dhiraj was seen clearly but the other guy was not seen. All moments of Dhiraj were noted but could not track any details of Shadow. Minnie then took the contracts signed by Dhiraj but could not get any details as he never signed any deal related to Shadow. Minnie asked Chirag, "how can he be so professional that he did not even make a single mistake?"

"Minnie, can you play the last meeting's video, it seems that I have seen the symbol?" replied Chirag.

As Minnie played the Video, Chirag saw it carefully and found the symbol. He then stopped the video and saw four guards around the main guy. Minnie played it again and both Mi-Chi noticed that one guard whispered something in Shadow's ears and then all started move towards the exit gate. Dhiraj was seen at that time when Shadow was leaving the place. He was the one who called who Shadow from behind. Both Mi-Chi were waiting for Shadow to turn around so that they could capture his face. Shadow turned back and the video ended. Minnie screamed, "yes, it was the same guy whom I saw in the army uniform. We finally found out the identity and the bee is trapped inside the place."

"Yes, it's a great achievement for us. And I think if dad finds out that it is our gadget then he will surely charge the bee by any method, and if not then crush it and throw it away." replied Chirag.

"Be positive always, we are getting close to him." Minnie smiled.

Satish shouted from the lab, "come here, kids. The bee's status is activated, come here fast."

Chirag saw that the bee was charged fully. "How can it be fully charged that too so quickly? He then turned on the camera and found his dad working with the wire. He understood that his dad had worked on it and charged it.

Chirag then directed the bee towards the air blower and reached out. He saw a guard walking towards the lift, so he flew the bee on the guard's helmet. The guard went up and moved towards the field and stood in a line. Chirag saw a lot of soldiers standing in a line and waiting for someone. An aircraft landed on the ground and the gates opened; two unknown creatures came out of the aircraft and were looking dangerous. Behind them, an alien was coming along with Shadow. A big truck with a container entered the main gate and the alien said something to Shadow pointing at the truck. The truck then turned in reverse direction.

Chirag noticed a cage nearby and flew the bee towards the cage and sat on the cage. He saw around 100 sheep in the cage and the cage was about 100 feet long. He thought that the truck would be carrying some food for the sheep. The moment the truck driver stopped and opened the container, fifty deadly alien creatures ran towards the sheep cage. The aliens teared them apart and ate as if they were hungry for years. They had a transmitter in their neck which was operated by the main Alien.

All three saw the video and were stunned at seeing the behavior. They all were frightened and Minnie screamed, "What the hell is all this? What are they doing here?"

"We heard about the same species when we went to find the device." replied Chirag. He then flew the bee upwards to find out where the place was. The alien who was standing on the entrance saw it and shot the bee with his laser gun. The bee was burnt in the air. Everything was gone. The last image captured by the bee was a big tree with a flag.

It was a nail-biting situation for all three.

"Are they going to feed our parents to them?" Chirag sounded helpless.

"Be brave. We will surely defeat them." Assured Minnie.

Minnie then decided to not send Satish in that grave danger. She realized that Satish Uncle was right when he said, "what happens, it happens for good." The bee got activated and we got to know about our enemy, but if we send uncle, it could be a suicide mission."

"Now we have to be more careful and take steps wisely." Said Minnie in a low tone.

Chapter 23
Task 3

Minnie brought the cube and pressed the button three. She took out the paper and a screen appeared displaying, 'so you managed to dodge the cops well, it's great to see our enemies well active, and we shall meet soon, all the best for your next target.'

It was a very easy task because no risk was assessed, therefore Minnie decided to go alone as she was sure to face this all by herself. "I don't want to put anyone of you in trouble, so I am going to do it alone and return safe." Asserted Minnie.

"Are you insane? Last time we decided not to take uncle and things changed, how can you take this step at this moment." Said Chirag.

"Minnie, Chirag is correct, we cannot predict what is going to happen next. I don't understand one thing: we completed two missions in a month and the other missions will be completed in a month or less, then why did he give us three months?" questioned Satish.

"I am not insane, it is that I care about you people and don't want you to get caught. And about the mission, all six tasks can be easily done in one month but the nuclear chemical will take ten days to get fully prepared for human trial." Replied Minnie.

"Then let's do it together and show our enemies that we are not cowards." Chirag smiled.

"Did we get any response from JOI?" Minnie asked Satish.

"No, we did not; I don't know why he is not replying to us." answered Satish.

"Ok, leave it now. We shall clear the task first and think about it later. We definitely need an army to fight with Shadow, it won't be that easy if I and Chirag fight alone." Minnie sat contemplating about the task.

"You always tell us to think positive and now you are the one talking negative. Don't be nervous, my dear. I have trust in both of you and you will surely win." Satish patted Minnie.

"Let's do it together but first we should make a full proof plan and move accordingly. We need to complete this in less than a week, till then I will get all the possible details." Replied Minnie

Chirag and Satish both agreed and went inside the lab. They were monitoring the device and also completing the gadget making.

Minnie, with the help of her source, got all the details of the next target. This time, Minnie asked the source to assign a man to follow the target and send her the details. The source assigned a local person who lived in Carlton City and instructed him to gather all the details. After a few days, Minnie got a call from her source asking her to meet. Minnie then called him to her home. The source reached home and Minnie called both Satish and Chirag and started the meeting.

"Mr. Noha, age 40 years, has a wife and one lovely daughter aged 15 years/ He gets up early at 5 am and starts the day by going on a walk in a park located 1 km away from his home with all his bodyguards. He returns home at 6 am, then goes to a yoga institute and returns home at 7 am. He freshen ups and at 7:30 am he has his breakfast. At 8 am, he reads newspaper and watches news channel for half an hour before going to the office. Sharp at 9 am, he reaches his unit and returns home at 5 pm. It is said that the liquid convertor was manufactured by his cousin and he liked the innovation so much that he purchased it in an auction by paying a huge amount and kept it in a craft room which is ten feet underground. If you need to enter the craft room, the only way is from the lift and to enter the lift you will surely require a fingerprint, eye scanner and a four digit combination code from which the lift gate will open and you will be able to move down. Mr. Noha is the purest man in the world, but every man has one weakness and for him it's his daughter. Even to enter his property is not that easy, in fact, no unknown person can enter his property. His servants enter a villa and get fully scanned before they enter the house. The house is fully guarded with CCTV camera and his camera room is also located under five feet and that is because once a hacker hacked his CCTV camera because it was outside. So, he has kept it underground, hardly any connection is found and to enter the room you will surely need to get through five cameras and you will certainly get caught because of the tight security at the place. If any unknown person tries to even enter the home, he would never be able to see his family again as he keeps that man as a slave in his factory and been watched with a security guard.

"Minnie, you wanted to go alone, right? Do you still wish to go alone?" asked Satish.

"As and when we decide to reduce a member, the risk gets double, and after hearing this, I am sure that yes, only I can do this and no one can stop me from going in." Minnie smiled.

"Don't even think of it. I forgot to mention the motion detectors which are placed from the main entrance to all over his place. If caught; you cannot imagine what's going to happen." Said the source

Minnie was frustrated, "uuuuhhhh…"

"Now also you want to go alone? Hahaha…" Chirag mocked Minnie.

The source then gave the full map of the home and the city, and left the place. Satish and Chirag went into the lab disappointedly, and Minnie started planning.

In the evening, Minnie explained her plan to Chirag and Satish. "The first thing is that we are not going to kidnap a fifteen-year-old girl and ask the machine in ransom. Second, if we go by air, we will be blown away. Third, if we go via water, the crocodiles will eat us and fourth, if we go by land, the guards will kill us. Now what I am planning is that we will dig the ground. Let's see if we have that option. As according to the map, all underground areas are covered with stainless steel sheets. For that, we have Chirag, he will melt it.

Next, how are we going to dig? Ok, let's see in the surroundings if we can buy a land and put a construction site symbol and start digging. Well, I did the research, so we have an empty land on the map which is 3kms away from the home and the property looks fine. Now, next, there is no water, sewage, or any kind of the line connected, so the way is clear. Also, we have two cameras; one on the left corner and one on the right corner, the craft room is around 1000sqft. and many stuffs are kept in it. We might get safe by hiding and as I can get invisible, I can get inside easily and bring the object.

So, the plan seems to be ok, right? Now I will call my source and buy the land on rent." Minnie takes her phone out and calls the source and said, "I have sent you a location and name of the land, so please see to it and but it by giving a token advance.

The source called Minnie after an hour and informed about the confirmation of the land. Minnie called Satish and Chirag in the hall and started to explain the plan; Satish was assigned to create a dummy construction company site and add dummy projects completed and get permission to dig the foreign land for construction purpose, and Chirag was said to get the bee and some gadgets along.

As usual, all promised not to harm anyone in the event and booked the tickets by different identities and moved to the airport.

It took two days to reach the Carlton city as air traveling took 20hrs and the further train traveling took 15 hours and rest in the hotel, so a total of two days were passed in reaching the destination. Till then, Satish was ready with the permission and Chirag was ready with the gadgets. All three, after reaching the destination, went to the site and hired some dummy construction site workers and made them act as if building something. They then brought big sheets and covered the area from all four sides. They also hired a manager to manage the cops or any department officer. The plan was set. Satish rented a medium size earth digger and brought it on the site. He then climbed on the machine and started to dig as per the plan. Minnie was guiding him from the back and he dig about 4kms. According to the map, the place was right next wall and so Minnie asked Satish to try to move a little further so that it could be easier for her. Minnie then tapped and a steel sheet sound was heard. She then told Chirag to use his fire balls and melt the sheet, it was so thick that it took him twenty minutes to melt. Minnie waited for ten minutes for the steel sheet to cool down as it was very hot. She then went invisible and took the gadget along with her. She began searching for the machine and found that it was exactly under camera and it could clearly be seen if she takes it. However, as she turned right, she realized that it was the wrong one and the actual machine was safe in another place and it was easy to steal it, so she moved towards the machine and took out the gadget. She resized the machine and took it along. All three safely came out of the pit and waited for the workers to fill it with the sand. They acted as if they wrongly dig the area. For workers, it took five hours to fill the pit. All three then paid the workers and the manager. Satish told that they were going for a meeting and may not come as the site was not fit for building. All the workers and the manager went off and the site was made to appear like before. The source too returned the documents and took back the advance by claiming that the land was not fit for construction. All three then booked a flight and reached home safely. This time Shadow did not disturb them, and that was not easy for them to digest. Anu reached home before they could reach. Satish was happy to see her wife.

"Now, three more tasks and four more people." Said Satish. They all then dispersed to their rooms.

Minnie was very disturbed and sat quietly in her room. Chirag knocked the door and went in.

"What happened?" asked Chirag.

"Nothing dude. I am just thinking of how can we arrange an army to defeat Shadow." replied Minnie.

"Don't worry, we will surely get help." Chirag assured.

"And how is that possible? JOI is not responding and whatever sources we had, we have utilized them enough. So, how are we going to manage, we have to arrange an army, if we don't get the army then we will not be able to defeat shadow." Replied Minnie

"You are our strength and you and I are more than an army, we will surely make a better plan and destroy Shadow. I trust you and you trust in God, everything will be fine. Now sleep well, we shall go to Dhiraj's house and figure out the dream you had months back. I think we can find something related to Shadow." Chirag smiled.

"I know. I was going to say the same and you spoke it. Getting smarter by staying with me, huh!" replied Minnie.

"Whatever! Now please sleep and don't think much. Did you keep the bee at place, you never discussed the dropping part and did anything go wrong?" Asked Chirag.

"No, nothing went wrong. This time, when I entered the code in the cube and the location that popped was nearby, so I went walking and waited for the Chopper. At the same time, I activated the bee and when I looked up searching for the chopper, it was next to me and I never noticed that. A gate opened, so I went inside it and saw no one was there; it was empty. I then kept the machine and resized it and suddenly when I got up, I felt as if someone was standing right behind me. When I turned back, no one was present. I was worried so I came out and when I came out and turned towards the chopper, an alien jumped down hiding above me. It was the same one who burnt our bee. The door closed and then I threw the bee, this time both landed in a gap but I was worried and scared after seeing the alien. It had yellow eyes and his structure of the face was like a Tassidermia Piranha with his big tongue coming out as if he wanted to taste me. His body was slim and was full black which cannot be seen easily in dark, and four arms with sharp claws. I am wondering why he did not kill me, was he sent to scare me?

Later when the chopper flew away, I was waiting to know the distance from the place where I was standing. When the numbers stopped, I saw it was just 700 km away from me, I think we are close enough."

"Was this your nightmare or you are trying to scare me?" asked Chirag.

"I wish you were with me." Replied Minnie.

"I would have roasted him. Well, jokes apart, we really need an army," said Chirag.

"Yes, this was the reason I was so disturbed." Replied Minnie.

"Share your thoughts with others, it will help you feel relaxed." Chirag smiled. "You have scared me and I will not be able to sleep." He giggled. "Anyway, I need to go to my room, I will listen to some music and get relaxed, you plan something." Chirag went away.

"Good night." Minnie smiled.

Chapter 24
Blessing

It was September 09, 2017,

The target date was 13th October 2017, one months and four days were left to execute the plan. Minnie woke up late at 9 am and went downstairs. She saw Chirag waiting for her.

“Had a good sleep?” Chirag smiled warmly.

“Hey, did you even sleep or are you waiting here since last night?” Minnie laughed.

“Come on. I am not afraid of anything. I will be prepared and yes, have your breakfast and let’s go to Dhiraj’s home.” Chirag smiled.

“Now that’s my brave man, we will surely figure it out, they don’t know with whom they are messing up.” Replied Minnie.

“Now that’s overconfidence.” Chirag smirked.

“I am confident and not overconfident.” Replied Minnie.

“Let’s see.” Said Chirag. They moved towards the door and Satish entered.

“Whoa… kids, where are you guys up to?” asked Satish.

Chirag explained everything and asked, “do you want to join?”

“No, you guys carry on. I will till then manage the lab work and keep an eye on JOI. And as you said the bee is activated, I will see if we find a hunch.” Satish smiled.

“Good idea uncle, see you soon.” Minnie waved a goodbye.

Minnie and Chirag went in the car and reached Dhiraj’s place. Minnie saw the place and stood outside the main door feeling emotional. Chirag told not to be emotional as it would make her weak. “Come on, we will not be able to focus for what we have come for.” Said Chirag hugging Minnie.

Minnie nodded and took out the keys and opened the lock. They both then entered the home. Minnie walked towards Dhiraj’s room and opened it. Both started to search everywhere but they forgot the main cupboard.

“Wait, what are we doing here? We need to open the cupboard.” Said Minnie.

"Yeah, actually we messed up the room." Chirag stood scratching his head.

Chirag opened the cupboard and began searching, "there's nothing here, and where did you see the tab?"

Minnie took all the clothes and shifted them to the left, but still found nothing. She thought she saw the tab there but now it wasn't seen. "Ok, wait. Let's try to move everything towards the right. Minnie then moved the clothes towards the right and a tab appeared in front displaying a screen, 'password.' Minnie typed her name and pressed enter. Suddenly, a door from the opened and a pure white light shone. Everything inside was so neat and arranged in a systematic way that a small lab was seen in right in front.

"I think all experiments were done here." Said Minnie.

Mi-Chi then started to look around if they find any clue related to Shadow. Minnie was walking towards a glass door through which she could see a stainless steel icebox, she then tried to open the glass door but it was asking a four-digit combination code which only Dhiraj knew. Minnie banged on the glass and said, "no man! We are so close and this happened. What would be the code?" She tried a few combinations made by her birthday and Dhiraj's lucky number. "This is the last attempt, if miss this, then the door will never open and a steel metal sheet will cover the place from all four sides." Minnie claimed after reading the disclaimer on the screen.

She sat down helplessly and tried thinking harder. She closed her eyes and tried to think. She suddenly got an intuition, 'Car.' She immediately opened her eyes but found no one around. "What could be the code with the car?" She took out her phone and opened notes. Next, she typed three car numbers; two were Dhiraj's and one was her favorite car. She was thinking which one should she type. She again closed her eyes and murmured, "Dhiraj's first car code was set for all his mobile-related devices and the other one was set for all the lockers, so what about the third one? Let's see if it had any other locks." She saw the door and said, "if the password is on my name, then the things inside would also be related to me only. Yes, so the code is 1905, my car's number, which is also my birth date." She then got up swiftly and entered the code. The door opened and Minnie began crying, "I love you, dad. I miss you, please come back soon."

Chirag heard her crying and ran towards her. "What happened? Are you fine?"

"I miss him so much" Minnie hugged Chirag.

"Ok, you may cry now and vent out all your pain. You will surely feel better." Chirag consoled her.

Minnie then saw towards the wall and said, "I can see Dhiraj waving at me and moving towards the wall."

"Where? I cannot see anything." Chirag looked carefully.

"Please hold him, he is leaving." Minnie started crying and sat on the floor helplessly.

Dhiraj stopped and everything froze. He was walking towards Minnie and said, “you are my strength, and the smartest person I ever meet. Don’t let yourself down and move on. I am always seeing you and I am near you. You will surely get success in your upcoming tasks, so please move on.” He kept saying move on and left the place slowly and disappeared.

Minnie screamed loudly while crying, “please don’t leave me alone.”

Chirag said with tears in his eyes, “it’s ok, please calm down.” He caressed her hair gently, consoling her.

Minnie stopped crying and saw in Chirag’s eyes and said, “nothing will happen to our parents and we will save them. The end of Shadow is confirm.”

“Now that’s like my strong sister” Chirag wiped his tears and got up. He gave his hand to Minnie and she held his hand and got up.

Minnie then moved inside the lab and opened the stainless-steel freezer box. She was stunned seeing the nuclear liquid which was supposed to be given to the lab.

“Ok, now I got it. That day when I gave the briefcase, he promised me that it would go in safe hands. He also knew that Shadow was already aware of Dhiraj and would plan an attack on him, and yes, that happened and Bozzo was sent to kidnap Dhiraj so that he could get the nuclear but that day you went and saved him. Our mom and dad are kidnapped because they did not get the nuclear glass inside the lab so they destroyed the nuclear building showing the world that nuclear is destroyed and no one can use it. And that day, when a message on cube appeared about the nuclear chemical, I was shocked seeing it and thought why was he asking for it as he was the one who destroyed it. He might have a hint about Dhiraj hiding it and so everyone is kidnapped. This is the reason Dhiraj replaced the nuclear glass with a dummy one and kept the original one inside the vault. That day, after our first task, you asked me, 'if everything can be done by Shadow so easily, then why does he need us to do the task?' This is the reason: **the 'Nuclear Chemical'**. He wants the chemical and he knows only I can bring that."

"It was all so planned and I always considered Dhiraj as a bad guy. I am wrong, he was a gem of a person. I really have respect for him in my heart." Chirag smiled.

Mi-Chi were fully clear about the objective of Shadow and went home happily. They explained everything to Satish and then all three started to make an exclusive plan to bring down Shadow and save their family.

"JOI, when are you planning to show up." Minnie whispered.